The final n...

As Samantha and Tor settled on the straw at the side of Pride's stall, Samantha could barely hold back the sobs that threatened to bubble up in her throat. She felt so choked up, she could hardly breathe as she gazed at Pride and remembered all their wonderful times together—the days caring for him when he was only a promising yearling; the hours they'd spent on the training oval, at the racetrack, and in the walking ring; the brilliant races he'd won and the cheering crowds. Even the disappointments of the races that were lost when the Townsends pressured him were memories she wanted to cherish. Most of all, though, she thought of the heart and courage Pride had always demonstrated and his sweet and loving personality. How she would miss him!

Don't miss these exciting books from HarperPaperbacks!

Collect all the books in the THOROUGHBRED series:

and the Super Editions:

Also by Joanna Campbell:

THOROUGHBRED

PRIDE'S
LAST RACE

JOANNA CAMPBELL

HarperPaperbacks
A Division of HarperCollins*Publishers*

This is a work of fiction. The characters, incidents, and dialogues are products of the author's imagination and are not to be construed as real. Any resemblance to actual events or persons, living or dead, is entirely coincidental.

HarperPaperbacks *A Division of* HarperCollins*Publishers*
10 East 53rd Street, New York, N.Y. 10022

Copyright © 1994 by Daniel Weiss Associates, Inc., and Joanna Campbell
Cover art copyright © 1994 Daniel Weiss Associates, Inc.

Produced by Daniel Weiss Associates, Inc., 33 West 17th Street, New York, New York 10011.

First printing: August 1994

Printed in the United States of America

HarperPaperbacks and colophon are trademarks of HarperCollins*Publishers*

10 9 8 7 6

PRIDE'S
LAST RACE

SAMANTHA MCLEAN BRUSHED DAMP TENDRILS OF RED HAIR off her face and chewed her lip worriedly as she glanced down the row of stabling at Saratoga Race Course. The backside of the racetrack was bustling on that hot August morning. Grooms bathed and walked horses and cleaned tack. Trainers and owners discussed the morning's workouts. Wonder's Pride, the beautiful chestnut Thoroughbred that Samantha groomed, stuck his elegant head over the stall door behind Samantha and touched his velvet nose to her shoulder. "No sign of them yet, boy," she said, giving his head an affectionate rub.

At that moment Pride's half-owner and trainer, Ashleigh Griffen, and her husband, Mike Reese, were attending a stewards' inquiry into the running of the Grade 1 Whitney Handicap, which Pride had won a few days before. Samantha was worried about the outcome. Ashleigh had lodged a protest against Brad

Townsend, son of the co-owner of Pride, for deliberately attempting to fix the race and ruin Pride's chances of winning. It was a serious offense that could result in Brad and his wife, Lavinia, being fined by the stewards and possibly barred from racing at Saratoga.

Finally Samantha saw Ashleigh's dark head and Mike's blond one as they approached down the row of stabling. She hurried to meet them. "How did it go?" she asked anxiously. Neither Ashleigh nor Mike looked happy.

"They got off," Ashleigh said, her hazel eyes flashing.

"What?" Samantha cried. "But how? I can't believe the stewards didn't at least give them a *warning!*"

"No fine. No warning," Ashleigh said.

It seemed impossible, when Samantha considered the extent of what Brad had done. Brad and Lavinia had raced their own horse—Lord Ainsley—in the Whitney, and he and Pride were major rivals. The evening before the race, when Pride's regular jockey, Jilly Gordon, had been forced to cancel, Brad hadn't bothered to tell Ashleigh. Instead he had assigned another, inexperienced jockey, Benny Alvero. Then Brad had given the jockey instructions about how to run the race—instructions that had totally contradicted Ashleigh's. The results had been nearly disastrous. Pride had won, beating Lord Ainsley after all, but he had come out of the race exhausted and dripping with sweat. It was nothing short of a miracle that he hadn't injured himself.

"Brad claimed Alvero misunderstood his instructions because his grasp of English is so poor," Ashleigh explained angrily.

"Brad shouldn't have been giving Alvero instructions in the first place!" Samantha cried. "Alvero should have listened to you—you're Pride's trainer and co-owner. Brad and Lavinia don't even own any interest in Pride. Mr. Townsend does!"

"Right," Ashleigh said, "but with Mr. Townsend away in England, Brad considers himself in charge of the Townsend Acres operation."

"But Alvero told you himself after the race that he could have ruined Pride by holding him back like he did," Samantha argued. "He was furious."

"Oh, I know," Ashleigh said. "Alvero told the stewards that he had understood Brad's instructions perfectly. He said that because he had only ridden in this country for Brad and Townsend Acres, he took Brad's instructions as the final say. He admitted that he hadn't paid any attention to me in the walking ring before the race when I told him to run Pride close to the lead."

"But I don't understand," Samantha said. "If Alvero backed you up, how could the stewards rule against you?"

"Because Alvero's English *is* terrible," Ashleigh said. "During the inquiry he had trouble answering all the stewards' questions without somebody translating for him."

"The stewards talked to us after the inquiry," Mike added. "They sympathized with us, but they had to conclude that there was a strong possibility

Alvero *had* misunderstood Brad. They didn't have any choice but to drop all charges against the Townsends."

"They did question why Brad had put Benny Alvero up as jockey in the first place," Ashleigh said. "You don't put an inexperienced jockey on a horse of Pride's caliber. The stewards weren't happy either that Brad hadn't told me that Jilly couldn't ride. Of course, dear charming Brad wiggled out of that one too, claiming he'd tried to reach me and couldn't get me on the phone."

Samantha discovered her hands were clenched in angry fists. This was only the last in a long line of irritations and problems Lavinia and Brad Townsend had caused Ashleigh. This was the closest Ashleigh had ever come to making them pay for their irresponsible actions. It absolutely infuriated Samantha that they had gotten off.

Mike put his arm around Ashleigh's shoulders. "Let's just hope that Brad and Lavinia will think twice about causing us any more trouble from now on. I don't think they'd get off so easy next time."

Samantha didn't have any high hopes about that. "What are you going to do?" she asked Ashleigh.

"There's nothing I really can do. We'll keep training Pride toward the Jockey Club Gold Cup in mid-October, then the Breeders' Cup early in November. Lord Ainsley will be racing in both of them, too. It's going to be pretty tense. If Pride wins both races, he's a shoo-in for Horse of the Year. Of course, if Lord Ainsley wins, then he'll get it."

"Lord Ainsley may be good, but Pride is the better horse," Samantha said loyally.

"Oh, I believe that, too," Ashleigh answered firmly. "Let's just hope everything goes smoothly between now and then."

Samantha glanced up to see her boyfriend, Tor Nelson, and her best friend, Yvonne Ortez, hurrying toward the stall. Tor was blond and blue eyed and trimly muscular from years of horseback riding. Yvonne had straight black hair and dark eyes, evidence of her Navajo-Spanish-English background. They had been over at the track watching the last of the morning workouts. Yvonne had driven up from Kentucky with Tor for the last two weeks of the Saratoga meet.

Tor came over to stand at Samantha's side. "So how did it go?" he quickly asked Ashleigh.

Ashleigh gave him the bad news.

"I don't believe it!" Tor shook his head angrily.

"That's disgusting!" Yvonne cried. "Now they'll really think they can get away with anything! Talk about unfair!"

"At least after tomorrow we won't have to see much of them," Ashleigh said with a sigh. "We'll be heading home. Boy, will I be glad to get back to Whitebrook!"

Samantha would, too. She loved the Saratoga track, with its turreted old grandstands, tree-shaded grounds, and homey atmosphere, but it had been a tense three weeks, and she missed the Kentucky farm where she, Ashleigh, and Mike lived.

"We'll have one last racing day tomorrow," Mike said. "Let's hope it will make up for today's catastrophe. I feel good about Sierra's chances in the first race."

"So do I," Tor agreed. Tor, who was a top-class show-jump rider, had been helping Samantha retrain one of Mike's three-year-old Thoroughbreds for steeplechasing. Sierra had won one steeplechase earlier in the Saratoga meet, with Tor jockeying him. "Although it's going to be a tougher race for him, since we moved him up in class. He'll be racing against more experienced horses."

"I'll be happy with a good showing," Mike said. "And I have two other horses running that Ashleigh will be riding—Miranda in the third race, and Blues King in the sixth."

"Miranda may be a disappointment," Ashleigh said, "but I think Blues King definitely has a chance of winning."

Mike nodded his agreement. "He sure isn't the prettiest horse I've owned, but he's turning into one of the best sprinters I've had."

"Don't Lavinia and Brad have a horse running in Blues King's race?" Samantha asked.

"Yup," Ashleigh said, "a gray three-year-old that they've been bragging about. He won a couple of races at other tracks, and as usual they're confident of a win, but I think they're going to be in for a surprise. They're not expecting a challenge from us. Blues King has only been lightly raced, but he keeps improving. Considering the workouts he's put in up here, I think he just might beat them. That would help take the sting out of the stewards' letting them off."

Suddenly Yvonne chuckled. Her dark eyes were twinkling. "I was just thinking of how we could let Brad and Lavinia know what we think of the ruling," she said. "I was picturing the front seat of Brad's precious Ferrari piled high with a steaming load from the muck pile."

Samantha gave a snort of laughter. She could just imagine Lavinia's haughtily pretty face if she opened the car door to *that*. "I love it!" She dissolved into giggles.

"Well, at least we can still see the funny side of things," Asleigh said, smiling herself.

Early the next afternoon Samantha, Yvonne, and Mike hurried up to their clubhouse seating as the field for the first race, the steeplechase, came out onto the track. Since Ashleigh was riding later that day, she was already in the jockeys' room.

Samantha crossed her fingers as she watched Tor ride out on Sierra. Tor looked so handsome in Mike's blue-and-white silks. He glanced up into the stands where they were sitting. Samantha smiled and blew him a kiss. He returned the smile, although Samantha could see he was growing tense as he mentally geared himself up for the race ahead.

Sierra, a big dark chestnut colt, tossed his head and pranced across the track, showing his usual high spirits. He'd been a willful colt, determined to have his own way, which meant he only ran when he felt like it. But he was a natural jumper, and once he'd been introduced to steeplechasing, he put his heart into it.

Yvonne looked up from her program and brushed her straight black hair from her cheek. "There are some good horses in the field," she said to Samantha. "That number-five horse, Magico, has won a couple of big 'chases."

"I know," Samantha said, "but Tor and I figured Sierra was ready for the challenge of better competition. The experience will be good for him. I'm not crazy about their post position, though—twelve, way on the outside."

"At least it will keep them clear of the scramble at the first fence," Yvonne said, "and Tor eventually will get Sierra up there close to the lead." For two years Yvonne had been taking lessons from Tor at his and his father's riding stable. She was turning into an incredibly good jump rider herself.

"Oh, I know Tor will give Sierra a good ride, but like you said, this is a much better field than in his last race."

Samantha glued her eyes to the gate as the horses finished loading. A second later the gate doors flipped open, and twelve Thoroughbred steeplechasers burst out onto the track. They headed away from the gate in a tightly bunched pack. Tor kept Sierra clear on the outside and only started angling the big horse over after the first fence, when the field had started to string out behind the two early leaders. The horses would go twice around the grass course, over sixteen hedgelike jumps in all.

As the field approached the third fence, Sierra and Tor were in fifth on the outside, with a tightly bunched group of riders inside of them. Sierra was tugging on the reins, anxious to go after the leaders, but if Tor let him out too soon, he wouldn't have anything left for the final fences of the two-mile race.

Tor and Sierra gradually moved up to fourth, Sierra gaining ground over the fences with his strong leaps. The five horse, Magico, was up in second, paced behind another favorite in the race. As the horses finished the first circuit, Sierra continued to edge up on the horse in third. "Come on, boy. Come on!" Samantha said under her breath as the field set off down the backstretch for the second time. The horse ahead of Sierra was tiring. Samantha gave a yelp of joy as Sierra caught him going over the next fence. A second later she gasped as she saw the tiring horse lose his footing as he landed off the fence. He stumbled sideways and went down on his knees. Tor had to haul back hard on the reins and swerve Sierra out and around the stumbling horse.

"No! That's done it!" Samantha cried miserably as four horses surged past Sierra on the inside before Tor had the big colt collected and in stride again.

"Bummer!" Yvonne said with a groan.

The near collision had cost them. Tor and Sierra were now back in seventh, but Sierra wasn't about to give up. Samantha could imagine the big colt's snort of fury that horses had passed him. Sierra powered forward, his strides eating up the ground between the fences. At least he and Tor were clear of the pack, but Samantha didn't hold out much hope that they could catch the leaders with only a quarter of the race yet to be run.

She cheered them on, though, as Sierra passed two horses between the next fences and bounded over the second-to-last fence, gaining another half-length. He was back up in fourth approaching the last fence. And as the leaders started sprinting to the wire, he moved into third, with the two favorites of the race still ahead of him.

"Go! Go!" Samantha cried as Sierra continued to gain, but she knew Sierra and Tor were going to run out of ground before they reached the wire.

They were still in third as they swept past the finish, but only a head behind the second-place horse. Sierra had put in a very impressive performance. They could all be proud of him. The track announcer seemed to agree. "Magico wins it, Hot Line second, and after a troubled trip, Sierra gets up for a fast-closing third. Looks like he's going to be a horse to watch!"

Samantha, Yvonne, and Mike hurried down to the gap to meet Tor as he rode Sierra off the track. "Good effort," another jockey called out to him.

"Thanks!" Tor answered. "Give him the credit, though."

Samantha held Sierra as Tor dismounted. "Good job, monster!" she affectionately told the horse, who was bobbing his head against her hold. She looked over to Tor, who smiled as he untacked Sierra.

"Did you see him take off after we avoided that

other horse? He surprised even me! Can you imagine where we might have been at the finish if I hadn't had to check him?"

"In first," Samantha said confidently. Tor leaned over and gave her a kiss on the cheek before heading off with his saddle to weigh in.

"That was a good start to the day," Mike said happily. "Let's hope the rest of it goes as well."

Two races later Ashleigh jockeyed Mike's filly, Miranda, up to a surprising second-place finish. As they gathered in the saddling paddock before the sixth race, in which Blues King would be running, Samantha hoped Whitebrook's good fortunes would continue. She saw Lavinia and Brad Townsend watching their entrant in the race, a nice-looking gray colt, as he was saddled. Samantha didn't know how they could stand there looking so innocent. They knew they were guilty of unethical behavior before the Whitney. They at least could have the decency to look a little bit ashamed. Samantha glanced up at Ashleigh as Mike gave her a leg into Blues King's saddle. Ashleigh looked assured and professional in Mike's silks, and she ignored Brad and Lavinia. Samantha saw Lavinia look over to Blues King as Mike led Ashleigh and the horse around the walking ring. Lavinia's piercingly arrogant voice cut through the air as she spoke to Brad. "Are they actually running *that* naggy-looking colt? They can't be serious."

Samantha smiled to herself. She hoped Lavinia would soon be eating her words.

Fifteen minutes later Samantha, Tor, Mike, and

Yvonne cheered from the stands as Ashleigh got Blues King out sharply from the gate to take the early lead. They never relinquished it. Instead, they left the rest of the field in the dust. Blues King won the sixth race by five lengths, with Lavinia and Brad's gray struggling to hold on to third.

"All right!" Samantha shouted. "That helps even things up!"

After Blues King's triumphant exit from the winner's circle, Yvonne jabbed Samantha with her elbow. "Did you see Lavinia's face after Blues King crossed the finish?" she asked Samantha with a chuckle.

"I did. She looked ready to spit."

"A good send-off for us," Yvonne said with malicious glee.

2

IT WAS LATE WHEN THEY ARRIVED BACK AT WHITEBROOK the following night. They had driven straight through from New York with only one stop to check the horses. "Home at last!" Tor said to Samantha and Yvonne, who had ridden in the van with him. Mike, Ashleigh, and Len were in the second van, carrying Pride and Mike's other horses.

"You must be exhausted after all that driving," Samantha sympathized.

"I'm pretty tired," Tor agreed. "And tomorrow it's back to work and class." Tor was starting his second semester at the Lexington branch of the University of Kentucky. In less than a week Samantha and Yvonne would begin their senior year at Henry Clay High.

Samantha saw the welcoming lights in the Reese farmhouse as they came down the long drive. Mike's father had watched over the breeding and training farm while they had been away. Mike had hired a new full-time groom, Vic Teleski, and several day workers to give him a hand. The new workers, though, didn't fill the void left after the death of Charlie Burke, who had passed away in July. The crusty old trainer had turned Pride and his dam, Ashleigh's Wonder, into champions and had taught Ashleigh everything she knew about training. They all still grieved over Charlie's death, and now Ashleigh alone bore the responsibility for training Pride and preparing him for two of the biggest races of his career. Samantha gave Ashleigh all the help she could. Not only was she Pride's groom, but she rode him in all his workouts. At sixteen Samantha had been exercise riding high-strung Thoroughbreds for three years, but Pride was special to her. She had been involved in Pride's training from the beginning, and he was clearly the most talented of all the horses she worked with.

Tor braked the van to a stop in the yard beside the stabling barns. Mr. Reese had turned on the spotlights. Samantha saw there were lights on in the cottage she shared with her widowed father, Ian McLean, the head trainer at Whitebrook. He'd driven back from Saratoga in his own car the day before and now hurried out of the cottage to give a hand with the unloading.

Beth Raines, the pretty, curly-blond-haired aerobics instructor he'd been dating all summer, followed him. Samantha felt a sudden stab of resentment at seeing Beth, then tried to push the feeling away. Beth had been in Saratoga with Mr. McLean and Saman-

14

tha. She had gone home early because of the increasing tension between her and Samantha, and her departure had left Samantha feeling guilty and childish. Beth had admitted that she'd edged into the McLean household too quickly, and Samantha knew the least she could do would be to give Beth another chance. And she would, she promised herself, though it wasn't easy accepting another woman in her father's life. She still felt the loss of her mother, who had been killed in a riding accident four years before.

She put Beth out of her mind, though, with the bustle of unloading the horses and getting them settled in their stalls. She led Pride into the training barn herself. Most of the sleek Thoroughbreds in the stalls were already dozing. A few snorted and stomped on their thick bedding.

A very happy white cat, with exotic black markings on his face that made him look like a bandit, was waiting outside Pride's stall. With tail high, the cat brushed against Samantha's legs, then, purring loudly, followed her and Pride into the stall. Pride lowered his head and breathed a greeting to the cat.

"Did you miss him, Sidney?" Samantha asked. "I think he missed you, too, but we couldn't take you up to Saratoga. He'll be home for a while now."

Sidney jumped up onto the stall partition to supervise as Samantha checked Pride's hay and water, removed his protective leg wraps and headgear, and adjusted the light sheet covering his back. Pride whuffed happily and rubbed his head against Samantha's shoulder.

"You're glad to be home, aren't you, big guy," she said softly as she took his elegant head in her hands and dropped a kiss on his nose.

Tor and Yvonne walked up to the stall. "Sierra's all set," Tor said, unsuccessfully hiding a yawn.

"Pride is, too," Samantha said as she gave Pride a last pat and let herself out of the stall. Sidney gracefully jumped from his seat on the partition onto Pride's back, where he curled up into a furry ball.

Tor put his arm around Samantha and gave her a hug. "I think I'm ready to call it a night. I'll drop Yvonne off on my way home. I'll see you tomorrow," he said.

Samantha laid her head against his chest and nodded. "Yvonne and I are going shopping for school stuff, but we'll stop by the stables afterward."

They all walked out to Tor's van. As Yvonne climbed into the passenger seat, Tor and Samantha exchanged a smile and a warm kiss. A moment later Samantha waved them off as Tor turned the van and headed up the drive.

Ashleigh walked up beside her. "We're finished for the night," she said. "Mike and I are heading in. I can barely keep my eyes open."

"Neither can I," Samantha admitted.

"I'll see you in the morning," Ashleigh said, "and thanks for all your help, Sammy."

Beth had left by the time Samantha went inside the cottage. Samantha said good night to her father, who was preparing to go up to bed himself. After brushing her teeth, she sleepily undressed and put on her nightgown, then crawled between the sheets. She sighed and closed her eyes, but as she drifted off to sleep, she couldn't help thinking of Brad and Lavinia's satisfied faces after the charges against them had been dropped. She had a feeling it wasn't the end of their problems with Brad Townsend and his wife.

"I can't believe we're starting our senior year," Yvonne said the next afternoon when they'd finished their shopping and were driving toward Tor's stable. Yvonne was behind the wheel. Samantha had failed her first driver's test over the summer shortly after Charlie's death. She'd been so upset, she had made some incredibly stupid mistakes and had been devastated when she didn't pass, but she would be practicing with Tor to try again.

"I know," Samantha agreed.

"We've really got to start thinking of colleges."

"Well, I've already made up my mind," Samantha said. "I need to stay close to home so I can work with the horses. I'm applying to the Lexington branch of the University of Kentucky."

Yvonne grinned. "I don't suppose it hurts that Tor goes there, too."

"That's not the reason I decided to stay in Lexington," Samantha said a little defensively, then smiled. "But you're right—it doesn't hurt."

"And with your grades, you're a cinch to get accepted. You could probably go anywhere you wanted. Me, that's a different story. Gregg is applying

17

all over the place," Yvonne said of her boyfriend of six months. "He wants to major in farm management and eventually turn his parents' land into a breeding farm. I'm not sure what I want to do—except keep riding and showing."

"You've got time," Samantha told her friend, "and if you keep your grades up this semester, I don't think you'll have any problem getting accepted anywhere."

Yvonne pulled into the drive of the Lexington stable Tor and his father owned and parked near the main stable building. The large indoor ring was behind the stable, and across the drive were two fenced outdoor rings. A class was in session, with Tor instructing. When he saw Samantha and Yvonne, he smiled and waved, then went back to his instruction. He was teaching an intermediate jump class, and Samantha and Yvonne paused to watch one of the students attempt a low gate and a two-fence combination. The student's mount balked at the combination, and Tor strode over. "Not enough leg," he called. "And keep your head up and eyes focused forward. You looked down and that threw off your approach."

They watched the rider try again and clear all the fences. "Let's go see Cisco," Yvonne said, anxious to see her regular mount after being away for two weeks. "One of the stable girls worked him on the longe line while I was in Saratoga, so he's stayed fit. I'm not going to give him a heavy workout today, but it'll feel good to get back in the saddle."

They entered the stable and walked along to

Cisco's stall. Most of the stalls were occupied by either school horses or privately owned horses boarded at the stable. Cisco whickered a happy greeting when he saw them. Yvonne grinned as she opened the stall door and gave the pure gray gelding a hug around the neck. "I missed you, fella. Yes, I brought you a carrot. After deserting you for two weeks, that's the least I can do." Tor and his father owned Cisco, but neither of them had the extra time to devote to his training. Yvonne had the time, and she needed a good mount, so for the last several months she'd been working with Cisco.

"Let's get you out in crossties and tacked up," Yvonne said as she gripped the gelding's halter and led him into the aisle. Samantha was waiting and clipped on the crossties, then reached up to give the horse's ears a scratch. Cisco loved it and gave a grunt of pleasure. As Yvonne brushed Cisco down, Samantha collected his saddle and bridle from the tack room. Within a few minutes they were leading the horse into the indoor ring.

Several jumps were already set up around the perimeter. Yvonne mounted, and Samantha watched from the sidelines as Yvonne warmed Cisco up at a walk, trot, and canter, then put him through some figure eights at a trot and canter. Samantha had taken jumping lessons from Tor herself, and that spring when Tor had broken his arm, she had ridden Sierra in his first steeplechase—a harrowing experience, although they had ended up doing really well. But her first love was training racehorses, and she knew she didn't have the natural skill at jumping that Tor and Yvonne had.

"He's looking good, Yvonne," she called to her friend. "He's really working smoothly. You've made a big improvement with him."

Yvonne smiled her thanks. "I think I'll try him over a few jumps. Would you mind raising the rail on that parallel?"

Samantha strode over to the fence Yvonne indicated and raised the top rail one notch so it stood about four feet off the ground. She returned to the side of the ring as Yvonne circled Cisco at a canter and headed him toward the first of the six fences, a low crossbar and rail. They skimmed over and cantered on to a brush, then the parallel, then a two-fence combination, and lastly Cisco gave a powerful leap over a wide fence painted to look like a stone wall.

"Perfect!" Samantha called. Tor walked up beside Samantha as Yvonne took Cisco through a second round. "They're looking good," she said to Tor.

"They sure are. I'm going to try to talk Yvonne into entering the National Horse Show in New Jersey this winter."

"You think they're ready?" Samantha asked. Tor and his Thoroughbred jumper, Top Hat, had won their division at the show the previous year, but Tor had been competing for years. Yvonne hadn't.

"I think they can be," Tor said, "if they keep working like they are."

"Wouldn't that be something!"

"Don't say anything to her yet, though," Tor told

her. "I'm going to wait until after she and Cisco compete in the Virginia show in October. Otherwise, I'm afraid she'll get too uptight."

"You and Top Hat are competing in that show, aren't you?"

Tor nodded. "In a different division, though. We lost a lot of practice time when I broke my arm last spring, but I think we'll be ready."

Yvonne and Cisco cleared the wall for the second time. Yvonne circled the horse, brought him down to a trot, and rode over to Tor and Samantha. "He's on his toes," she said with a smile.

"So are you," Samantha said.

Yvonne dismounted and pulled up her stirrups. "I meant to ask you two what you were doing Sunday. I thought I'd invite myself and Gregg over to Whitebrook for a trail ride."

"I'd love it," Samantha said, "but Tor and I promised Beth we'd go to a field day for disabled children that her health club helps sponsor. Beth's really active in the organization, and after the way I acted toward her in Saratoga, I really feel like I should go. But I'm sure Mike and Ashleigh wouldn't mind if you and Gregg went on a ride by yourselves."

"Maybe we will," Yvonne said.

Since Tor had another class to teach, Yvonne drove Samantha back to Whitebrook. As Samantha waved Yvonne off she saw they had a visitor. Clay Townsend's Jeep Cherokee was parked near the barns. *So he's finally back from England,* Samantha thought. She couldn't wait to find out his reaction to his son and daughter-in-law's stunt before the running of the Whitney. She hurried in the direction of the training barn, guessing that Ashleigh and Mr. Townsend would be at Pride's stall.

They were. "I realize you're angry, Ashleigh," Mr. Townsend was saying, "and I truly am sorry about the misunderstanding. So is Brad. In any case, it turned out well in the end. Pride won."

Samantha saw Ashleigh grimace. Mr. Townsend obviously had bought Brad and Lavinia's version of the story if he believed their interference had been an accident.

"He looks like he's come out of the race well, too," Mr. Townsend continued. "You're giving him a week's rest?"

"Yes," Ashleigh said. "Then he'll have a month's solid training before the Gold Cup."

"Lord Ainsley will be running in the Woodward in two weeks," Mr. Townsend said thoughtfully. "I know Pride doesn't like a heavy race schedule, and I don't want to push him, but do you think just the one prep race before the Breeders' Cup is going to be enough?"

Samantha noticed the flash of uncertainty that crossed Ashleigh's features. She knew how heavily Ashleigh felt her responsibilities and missed Charlie's advice and wisdom. Her inexperience as a trainer had already been questioned by others. Some of those doubts had been laid to rest with Pride's victory in the Whitney. Still, Ashleigh would be held responsible for Pride's success or failure. "Two big races before the Breeders' Cup could take too much out of him," Ashleigh said. "I want him to be as sharp as he can be for the Classic."

Mr. Townsend pursed his lips. "I'll leave it to you, then. I'd just as soon not have the two horses racing against each other more than necessary. It creates too much of a conflict." He paused. "I'll be leaving for England again in a week and will probably be away until just before the Breeders' Cup. I'll keep in touch." Even as he spoke Samantha had the feeling that his thoughts were more on his business on the other side of the Atlantic.

After Mr. Townsend left, she said sourly to Ashleigh, "So I guess Brad and Lavinia have covered their tracks."

"I suppose it was silly to expect anything else." Ashleigh frowned. "Brad's his son, so Mr. Townsend is bound to believe his story. At least we won't be racing against them in the Woodward. We'll just have to hope they stay out of our hair before the Jockey Club Gold Cup."

3

ON SUNDAY, SAMANTHA AND TOR WATCHED FROM THE sidelines as a dozen wheelchair-bound children raced down the Lexington athletic field toward the red tape strung across the finish line. "Wow," Samantha said. "I don't think I could get a wheelchair to move that fast."

"They're pretty amazing," Tor agreed. "It kind of makes you feel humble."

"And they look like they're having so much fun!" Samantha said. Dozens of others sat on blankets spread on the grass along the edge of the field as the children's field day neared its end. Beth had helped to organize the activities, and she and Samantha's father had spent the previous hours at the far end of the field preparing children for their events. Not all the children were in wheelchairs, but all of them had some sort of physical disability. There had been foot-races, a relay, a sack race, a potato race, and ball tosses. The wheelchair race was the last event.

Samantha and Tor rose as the race ended in a dead heat to cheers from the crowd. They headed toward the awards stand, where ribbons for all the events would be presented. They found Beth and Mr. McLean and another of the field day organizers, Janet Roarsh, a physical therapist. Beth's face was flushed from excitement and pleasure. She ran her fingers through her short blond curls. "It went well, don't you think?" she said to Samantha and Tor. "I just wish every one of them could win, but since that's not possible, we're going to give a participant's ribbon to each child. That way each of them will know they've done something special."

Samantha couldn't help but be impressed at the energy and enthusiasm Beth had put into the day's events and into helping the children. She was seeing a side of Beth she hadn't seen before. "I don't know if I'd have the guts to get out there and try the way these kids did," Samantha said. "They're amazing."

A shadow crossed Beth's face. "Well, you don't always see the smiles you're seeing today. They get frustrated and depressed, especially the children who developed problems later in life. They can't understand why they can't do the things they used to do anymore."

"A day like today lifts your spirits, though," Janet said. "It's a shame we can't do field days more often, but it takes a lot of work to put together an event like this. I think the most frustrating part for the children is their lack of mobility—their dependence on a wheelchair or braces and crutches."

Tor was frowning thoughtfully. "Could they ride?" he asked Janet. "Horses, I mean—actually ponies—with someone leading them?"

"I know it's been done," Janet said, "but we don't have the facilities."

Tor glanced over to Samantha, his blue eyes bright, and lifted his brows in question. Samantha nodded, understanding Tor's train of thought. "I have the facilities," he said. "My father and I have a riding stable here in Lexington."

"That's right!" Janet said. "Beth has told me you're all horse people. But we couldn't afford it—"

"Well, I'd be willing to donate the use of the ponies and the ring," Tor said, "and some time. I think Sammy would, too."

Samantha nodded in agreement. "And I have a couple of friends who might be willing to help."

"Of course, you couldn't have too big a class," Tor added. "Maybe six at a time, and have the class meet once a week or every other week. Could you get them to the stable?"

"That's no problem," Janet responded, her eyes beginning to shine with excitement. "We have a van. I'd have to have their parents' permission first, and I'd have to look into insurance."

"I think it's a wonderful idea!" Beth said. "I'm sure we could work something out, Janet—not that I know anything about horses, but Tor and Sammy are experts."

Tor laughed. "I don't know about experts, but we've had plenty of experience."

"Well, I'd be delighted to consider it and do what I can from my end," Janet said. "The hard part will be deciding which children to ask to participate. Can I call you during the week to make arrangements?" she asked Tor.

"If I'm not there, just leave a message, and I'll get back to you."

"Are you two sure you want to get involved in all this?" Janet asked, giving both Samantha and Tor a searching look.

"If it will help make a few children happier," Samantha said, "it will be worth it."

"Thank you, and I *will* be in touch!"

On the way home Beth turned to Samantha and Tor with a glowing expression. "That really was a great idea. Thank you both. I don't think you'll be sorry."

Again Samantha reconsidered her impressions of Beth. Maybe she hadn't given Beth a fair shake.

When Samantha hurried into Henry Clay High on Tuesday morning for the first day of her senior year, the halls were already crowded. She called and waved greetings to kids she knew. She noticed many new and sometimes bewildered faces in the halls, too—the incoming freshman class.

Yvonne and Maureen O'Brien, the editor of the school newspaper and another good friend of Samantha's, were waiting for Samantha at her

28

locker. Maureen, who was no more than five feet tall, already clutched a pile of notebooks in her arms.

"I was sorry to hear about Charlie," Maureen said sadly to Samantha. "You guys must miss him."

"We sure do," Samantha said. "I still keep expecting to see him walk out of the barn."

Maureen nodded her understanding. "You could write a tribute to Charlie for the school paper," she suggested. "Everyone who's read your column knows what a great trainer he was."

"That's a great idea," Samantha said. "I'd love to do it, if I can find the time."

"You have a couple of weeks before the deadline for the first issue. Sounds like the rest of your summer was pretty busy," Maureen added. "Yvonne was telling me all about Saratoga and about Ashleigh and Mike's wedding."

"Things weren't boring, that's for sure," Samantha said. "How'd you like your job at the newspaper?" Maureen had taken a summer job at one of the local papers, hoping to get a taste of real journalism.

"All they gave me was grunt work," Maureen said with a frown. "I didn't get to write a thing."

"Guess that's what they call working your way up the ladder," Yvonne teased.

Maureen wrinkled her snub nose. "At least I got to see how a newspaper operates, and they want me back during vacations. I guess I'll have to do all my writing for the school paper. Who did you get for English?" Maureen asked Samantha. "I was hoping we'd be in the same class again."

"Mr. Schneider," Samantha said.

"Me too!" Maureen answered. "Who'd you get for trig?"

Samantha made a face. "Mrs. Gilmore. From everything I've heard, she's tough."

"But you'll manage to get at least a B, I'm sure," Yvonne said. "I'm the one who really needs to get my grades up this year."

"Don't worry, Maureen and I will give you a hand if you need it," Samantha told her.

"Right!" Maureen agreed. "We'll lock you in a room and stand over you with a whip." They all laughed as they moved up the crowded hallway to their respective homerooms, promising to meet at lunch.

The day flew by, and after the last class, Yvonne offered to give Samantha a ride home. "Not a bad day," Yvonne said as they drove to Whitebrook. "I can't complain about any of my teachers except sourpuss Sorrenson, and it was great to see everyone again. Did you talk to Anne Hedgegrove? She spent the whole summer at a riding camp in Vermont. Boy, was I jealous. She didn't even have to pay for it. A friend of her family runs the camp."

Samantha grinned. "You don't need to go to a fancy riding camp. You're doing great right here in Lexington, and I'll bet the coaches at those camps aren't any better than Tor."

"Yeah, I guess," Yvonne agreed. "But it still sounded pretty cool."

Yvonne stayed for a few minutes when they reached Whitebrook. Samantha immediately checked on Pride, who was grazing in a small paddock, enjoying his time off. She gave him a loving look but didn't disturb him, letting him eat his fill of the lush grass. A few paddocks over, the mares and foals were grazing. As Samantha and Yvonne leaned against the paddock fence, a beautiful chestnut mare looked in their direction, whickered, and trotted eagerly toward them. Her four-month-old foal, Mr. Wonderful, gamboled after her.

"Hey, Wonder," Samantha greeted the former champion mare as she reached up a hand to affectionately rub Wonder's neck. "How are you today, girl?" Samantha dug in her pocket and produced some broken carrot bits, which Wonder gratefully accepted. Her chestnut foal pushed forward eagerly. Samantha laughed. "Yes, I've got something for you, too, little guy." Mr. Wonderful was Wonder's third foal. Her first offspring was Pride, who had been foaled four years earlier. Her only other foal was a filly, Townsend Princess, due to begin her yearling training that fall. Unfortunately Clay Townsend, who was not only half-owner with Ashleigh of Wonder and Pride but of all of Wonder's foals, had wanted Princess to do her training at Townsend Acres. The young filly was stabled there. Ashleigh wasn't happy about it, but there was nothing she could do, since Mr. Townsend had agreed to let her keep Wonder and Pride at Whitebrook. Ashleigh was hoping he'd agree to let Mr. Wonderful remain at Whitebrook for his eventual training.

Samantha whistled for Ashleigh's nearly black former race mare, Fleet Goddess, who was grazing at the far side of the paddock with her foal, Precocious. Fleet Goddess raised her head in response to the whistle, pricked her ears, and started across the paddock with the lively black filly in her wake. Both Wonder and Fleet Goddess were in foal again and would deliver in the spring.

"So these little guys are going to be weaned this weekend," Yvonne said of the foals.

"Yes. The foals get pretty upset when they're separated from their dams, so Ashleigh and I will stay with them until they calm down. It usually only takes an hour before they start playing with each other and forget how miserable they are."

"Have you heard when they're starting yearling training over at Townsend Acres?" Yvonne asked.

"No, but Hank will let us know. He's in charge of the yearlings, and he and Len talk all the time. Hank keeps an eye on Princess for Ashleigh."

"Do you think Townsend Princess is going to have the same kind of talent as Wonder and Pride?" Yvonne asked.

"It's too soon to tell, but her conformation is perfect, and from what Ashleigh says, she's a very intelligent filly. She's showing all the signs of being a potential winner. Of course, it bothers Ashleigh that she's not going to have any real control of Princess's training."

"Who will have control?" Yvonne asked. "Ken Maddock?"

"As head trainer, he should. I'm just afraid that Brad and Lavinia might try to butt in."

"You think they might? Lavinia sure doesn't know anything, and I didn't think Brad took much interest in the training until the horses were closer to racing age."

"He usually doesn't, but you know how much Lavinia hates it that Ashleigh has been in charge of Pride. I wouldn't be surprised if she took a big interest in Princess, just out of spite. She's got to know how much it would upset Ashleigh. She's so jealous of Ashleigh and everything that Ashleigh's done, I wouldn't put anything past her."

"Scary," Yvonne said. "I can't believe there are people who actually feel sorry for her. I mean, it's tough being an only child whose mother practically deserted you, but that's no excuse for expecting to have everything go your way."

"Lavinia's father spoiled her rotten to make up for her mother," Samantha said. "She always got what she wanted. He gave her anything money could buy, and he has plenty."

"And now she expects everyone else to do the same," Yvonne said sourly. "I can't feel sorry for her. She's just like Brad. Both of them have egos as big as balloons."

Samantha chuckled. "That's why they get along so well. And you know she and Brad can turn on the charm when they want to."

"It would be terrible if Brad decided to take over Princess's training."

"I know," Samantha said. "But who could stop him? His father's in England, and while Mr. Townsend is away, Brad's in charge—and that means Lavinia will have plenty to say, too."

"Yuck! Poor Ashleigh."

"Don't worry about Ashleigh. She's not going to let them walk all over her again," Samantha said.

EARLY SATURDAY MORNING, SAMANTHA SADDLED UP PRIDE and took him out for a ride over the trails. He would be going back into intensive training soon to prepare for the Jockey Club Gold Cup, but Samantha thought a relaxed ride that morning would do them both good. Pride certainly was eager as Samantha trotted him up one of the grassy lanes between the paddocks. "It's great to be out here, boy, isn't it?" Samantha said with a smile.

Pride snorted his agreement as Samantha urged him into a canter. The day was clear, with the first nip of fall in the morning air. Samantha breathed deeply and relished the breeze against her cheeks. Pride's warm breath misted in the cooler air. His cantering strides carried them effortlessly past white-fenced paddocks, where a few horses were already grazing. They swept along over the lush grass from one end of Whitebrook to the other. Samantha felt as free as a bird, as if she and Pride had taken wing. As always she thrilled to Pride's powerful strides and fluid grace. She let him out into a slow gallop and they pounded over the turf, with Pride's hoofbeats and evenly snorted breaths echoing in Samantha's ears. Pride's mane whipped back in her face as she leaned close over his neck.

These were the times when Samantha wished she hadn't grown so tall. She longed to actually jockey Pride in a race, but she had to face the facts. At five foot five and a hundred and eighteen pounds, she was too big to be a professional flat-racing jockey. She would have to content herself with these moments, and her hours riding Pride on the training oval.

Samantha could have ridden for another hour, but the foals were being weaned that morning and she'd promised to give Ashleigh a hand. Pride barely seemed winded when Samantha turned him to head back to the stable yard. "That was fun, wasn't it, fella?" Samantha asked breathlessly. "I can see you're ready to start training for the Gold Cup, but I love it when we can just go out and play around." Pride tossed his head. "You're so gorgeous, but I think you know it," Samantha teased.

Ashleigh was waiting when Pride and Samantha trotted back into the yard. "Looks like you two had a good time," she said with a smile.

"We did. He loved being out there." Samantha dismounted. "Look at that—he's barely worked up a sweat."

Len walked over as Samantha removed Pride's

saddle. "Want me to cool him out for you?" he asked. "I know you want to help with the weanlings."

"Thanks, Len. I'd appreciate it." Samantha gave Pride's shoulder a last pat. "See you later, big guy."

Mike's father and Vic were already leading two mares and their foals from the barn as Samantha and Ashleigh approached. As the men led off the mares to one paddock, Samantha and Ashleigh took the foals' halters and brought them to a different paddock.

It was a chaotic scene. The foals called anxiously as their dams were led off. They fought frantically against the hold on their halters.

"Easy, babies," Samantha soothed. She hated to see their distress, but she knew from experience that they would soon calm down. The foals were past the point where they needed to nurse, and their dams would soon have discouraged them from nursing anyway. As Ashleigh and Samantha released the foals, they raced across the grass to stand at the fence closest to the paddock where the mares had been led. There were eight foals in all, including Precocious and Mr. Wonderful.

"Maybe I'm prejudiced," Ashleigh said as they followed the foals across the paddock, "but Mr. Wonderful and Precocious really stand out from the others, don't they? I think they're both going to be special horses like their moms."

"I think so, too," Samantha agreed as her eyes picked out Precocious and Mr. Wonderful. Both foals were alert and lively and full of mischief—traits that Ashleigh and Samantha hoped would someday develop into a love of racing and winning. "They're good buddies, too. I've noticed they always pair off to play together."

Ashleigh smiled. "A good combination." They had reached the clustered foals and called out soothingly to them. Precocious and Mr. Wonderful turned and trotted toward the young women. Their heads were now as high as Samantha's, and they would continue to grow in leaps and bounds. But neither of the foals was happy at the moment. They nudged Ashleigh and Samantha with their noses, then turned to gaze in the direction of the mares' paddock and squealed anxiously.

Samantha rubbed Precocious's still-fuzzy black mane. "I know, sweetie," she said. "You want your mom, but you'll be okay on your own—and you've got Mr. Wonderful and all the other foals to play with." The filly flicked her oversize ears, but still gazed toward the other paddock and her mother.

"What you guys need is a little distraction," Ashleigh said to Mr. Wonderful. "How about a race? Come on." She turned and did a few jogging steps across the pasture. Samantha did the same. The two foals looked at the girls, then back at the fence. They were obviously torn between their longing for their dams and the prospect of play. Samantha jogged back to the foals, patting them lightly on the rump. "Come on! Let's go for a run!" She jogged off again, and now the foals followed, scampering on their long, knobby-kneed legs. Just as the foals caught up with them, Ashleigh and Samantha picked up speed. The foals came in pursuit, and now their attention was fully directed to the game.

The young women and foals ran in circles and loops over the grass in a version of tag. Soon the remaining foals left the fence and started trotting over to join in the fun.

Samantha and Ashleigh were laughing and breathless when they finally plopped down on the grass, conceding victory to the much speedier foals. Precocious and Mr. Wonderful ambled over, both of them tossing their heads happily. Samantha and Ashleigh reached up to rub their noses.

"Feeling better now, guys?" Samantha asked. "You sure tuckered me out. It wasn't really any contest, was it?"

"Wouldn't it be great if these two had a foal one day," Ashleigh said musingly.

Samantha chuckled. "You're really planning ahead, aren't you? They have a long way to go before that. They won't even begin their training until next fall."

Ashleigh returned Samantha's smile. "I know, but it doesn't hurt to dream. Dreams always keep me going. I had these incredible dreams for Wonder and Pride when they were foals."

"And they've lived up to your dreams," Samantha said.

"They sure have. Even if Pride doesn't win the Classic, he's given me some pretty amazing moments. So has Wonder. I wouldn't trade it for anything." Ashleigh rose and brushed off her jeans. "I think they'll be all right now. Are you going to come by the house to watch the Woodward this afternoon?" she asked Samantha.

"I wouldn't miss it. Tor's coming by, too. Do you think Lord Ainsley will win?"

"Unless there's some kind of an upset. With Pride not running, Lord Ainsley is definitely the best horse in the field. In a way I'd like to see him win," Ashleigh added. "I don't have anything against the horse—only his owners."

"But he's Pride's main competition!" Samantha exclaimed.

Ashleigh laughed. "I'm only talking about *this* race," she clarified. "I sure don't want him winning any races against Pride!"

When Samantha returned to the cottage, she found that a card from the motor vehicle department had come in the mail. She'd been given another appointment for her driver's test—in less than a week. *Oh, my God,* she thought, *I've got to practice! I'm not going to fail this one!*

Tor knocked on the door a few minutes before the race was to start. "I just got a call from Janet Roarsh," Tor said when Samantha let him in. "I wanted to check with you first, but we've tentatively set a time for the first session with the disabled riders. Does Wednesday afternoon sound okay to you? Janet and Beth have talked to all the parents involved and gotten their permission. She said they would be bringing six children."

"Wednesday sounds great to me. I'll call Yvonne

and see if she can give us a hand. I got news today, too," Samantha said. "They gave me another appointment for my driver's test—in less than a week! How am I going to be ready?"

Tor laughed and gave her a reassuring squeeze. "Don't panic. We'll have you ready. You know you only messed up the last time because you were so upset after Charlie died."

And she'd also been angry about Beth suddenly appearing in her father's life, but Tor didn't know that. "I'm going to be even more nervous this time," Samantha said. "What if I fail the test *again*?"

"You won't. I'll take you out this afternoon after we watch the race, okay?" He gave her a warm look, which Samantha returned with a smile.

It was silly, she knew, to get so nervous. She wasn't frightened when she was galloping horses around the track, and that required far more skill and was far more dangerous. But nearly all the kids her age had their licenses. She'd feel like a total idiot if she couldn't manage to get hers.

Samantha and Tor crossed the stable yard to the Reese house.

"Come on in," Ashleigh called in response to their knock. "I'm in the living room."

They walked into the big, comfortably furnished room. Ashleigh had turned on the TV and was adjusting the focus. The Woodward would be run at Belmont in New York. As the network commentator gave a rundown of the field and the prerace conditions, the camera panned over the big Bel-

41

mont track. The sky was a leaden gray.

"Not the best conditions for the running of the Woodward," the commentator said. "The rain stopped about an hour ago, but the track is still listed as sloppy. We've spoken to the owners and trainer of the favorite in the race, Lord Ainsley, but they have no plans to scratch the horse because of the track conditions."

"Does Lord Ainsley like the mud?" Tor asked.

"He hasn't raced in the mud here," Ashleigh answered, "but he was used to soft going on the turf in England before Lavinia bought him and shipped him over here. He liked it enough that he was the English three-year-old champion."

"Lewiston, the five horse, likes the mud," Samantha said, "but he's not in the same league as Lord Ainsley."

They sat down to watch as the cameras switched to a shot of the saddling paddock and walking ring. The eight horses in the Woodward had been tacked up and were being led around the ring. The camera zoomed in for a close-up of Lavinia and Brad. Both of them smiled graciously for the benefit of the cameras, making Samantha's stomach turn. But a second later the camera refocused on the field as the horses, with jockeys up, headed out to the track.

Mike came in and sat down beside Ashleigh as the horses were loaded into the gate, Lord Ainsley in the four slot. At the bell Lord Ainsley broke sharply and settled in just off the lead. He remained there as the field went around the first turn and down the backstretch.

"Looks like it's pretty heavy going," Mike said.

Samantha knew what it would be like for the jockeys on such a sloppy track, and she didn't envy them. Mud would be flying in their faces, coating them and their goggles and making it difficult to see. Their mounts would have trouble grabbing the slippery surface.

But Lord Ainsley and his jockey, LeBlanc, were bearing on. Near the end of the backstretch they began moving up on the lead horse, and as the field went into the far turn Lord Ainsley took the lead. It should have been clear sailing for him from there to the wire, but at the top of the stretch Lewiston, the horse who loved the mud, started making a bid, moving up on Lord Ainsley's flank and really pressuring him. On any other racing surface Lewiston wouldn't have stood a chance against Lord Ainsley, but for a moment it looked like Lewiston would actually go right on by.

LeBlanc went to his whip. Lord Ainsley responded and struggled on. Lewiston continued challenging. The two horses battled neck and neck down the stretch, leaving the rest of the field behind. It was obvious Lord Ainsley was giving it everything he had, fighting through the heavy going of the sloppy track. He managed to keep his head in front as they went under the wire.

"Whew!" Samantha said, admiring the courage Lord Ainsley had just shown. "That had to have taken a lot out of him. I don't think LeBlanc was seriously expecting to be challenged."

"No," Mike agreed. "Lord Ainsley's definitely shown he has heart. It remains to be seen how he'll come out of the race."

They continued to watch as Lord Ainsley and LeBlanc, both liberally splattered in mud, rode into the winner's circle. Brad and Lavinia were already there. Samantha noticed that Lavinia stayed well away from her mud-covered horse. *God forbid he should dirty her designer clothes,* Samantha thought. The TV anchor questioned them. "So after today's victory," he asked, "how do you feel about your chances in the Breeders' Cup?"

"We feel very good about our chances in the Breeders' Cup," Lavinia responded with a charming smile. "Lord Ainsley put in a remarkable effort today, especially considering the condition of the track. He's shown what a versatile horse he is."

"Like she knows what she's talking about," Ashleigh muttered. "What a phony."

"And what are your plans before the Breeders' Cup?"

Brad responded this time. "If all goes well, we'll be running in the Jockey Club Gold Cup."

"Wonder's Pride is also running in the Gold Cup," the anchor said. "With him and Lord Ainsley vying for honors as top handicap horse, how much of a threat do you see him posing?"

"I'm frankly not concerned," Brad said smoothly. "Lord Ainsley is improving off each race. Wonder's Pride won't have raced in nearly two months coming into the Gold Cup. A fairly long layoff. Of course, although both horses race in Townsend

44

Acres' colors, I have no control over Pride's training and race schedule."

"You creep!" Ashleigh cried, rising and turning off the set.

"It's only Brad-speak," Mike told her. "You know better than to let it get to you."

"It just infuriates me that he can't resist getting in a gibe whenever he can. I am doing the right thing, aren't I? My instincts are not to overrace Pride. The Gold Cup should be enough of a prep for the Breeders' Cup. But if he loses the Gold Cup . . . and there's Horse of the Year honors to think about—"

"Ash, relax!" Mike said. "You're doing the right thing. If you start doubting yourself, you'll be playing right into Brad's hands."

"Brad and Lavinia are the ones who are taking a risk. They may be overracing Lord Ainsley," Samantha told Ashleigh. "Pride's going to be the fresher horse on Breeders' Cup day."

Ashleigh heaved a sigh. "I know. I just miss Charlie's advice so much. I keep thinking that if Pride doesn't win his next two races, everyone's going to point the finger at me."

"That won't happen," Samantha said, and prayed she was right.

They were all anxious to hear how Lord Ainsley had come out of the race, since it could affect his performance in the Gold Cup when he ran against Pride. Early the following week, Ken Maddock, the head trainer at Townsend Acres, stopped by to visit Samantha's father and Mike. Maddock had been Ian McLean's boss when the McLeans had lived at Townsend Acres, and the two men had remained friends.

Samantha arrived home from school to find the men talking in the stable yard. She walked over.

"It was heavy going in that slop," Maddock was telling her father, "and I didn't think we'd be running neck and neck down the stretch."

"Lord Ainsley put in an impressive effort," Mr. McLean commented.

"He did run an incredible race," Maddock agreed, "but if it were up to me, I'd think twice about running him in the Gold Cup. Normally he's a horse who doesn't mind a heavy race schedule, but he ran his heart out in the Woodward and could use more of a rest before the Breeders' Cup. I don't have to tell you that it would be the high point of my career if Lord Ainsley won the Classic." Maddock chuckled. "Though I guess I'm talking to the wrong person about that. You'll have all your bets on Pride."

Ian McLean smiled and looked over to Samantha. "With Sammy's involvement, that shouldn't be surprising. But this is horse racing. You can be adversaries and friends at the same time."

I wonder if anyone's told Brad and Lavinia that? Samantha thought.

"Anyway," Maddock said, "I'll be pointing Lord Ainsley to the Gold Cup. Lavinia and Brad won't hear of pulling him out—if he wins it, it will put him one win ahead of Pride and that much closer to Horse of the Year." Maddock frowned. "We'll see. He has started to snap back, and we still have a couple of weeks before the next race."

SAMANTHA, TOR, YVONNE, AND GREGG HAD SIX GENTLE-mannered ponies tacked up and ready to go on Wednesday afternoon when Beth and Janet escorted the young children into the indoor ring of the stable. Three were in wheelchairs, two were on crutches, and a little black girl was on crutches and in leg braces from ankle to knee. All the children looked around in awe at the huge indoor arena, then at the ponies lined up to one side. None of them looked older than seven. Tor and Samantha walked over to greet them.

"We're all set to go," Beth said with a smile. "Tor and Samantha are going to help you learn to ride, so please listen to them carefully. If everyone cooperates, I'm sure we're going to have a lot of fun. Now Tor can explain what he wants you to do."

"It's not going to be hard," Tor said. "We'll put you up in the saddle. Today all you'll have to do is hold on. We'll lead the ponies around, so there's nothing to be afraid of, but if any of you want to stop at any time, just tell us. Are you ready?"

Six small heads nodded.

"We'll bring the ponies over here. Yvonne and Gregg are going to help." Tor introduced them. "Beth, do you think you and Janet could each lead a pony?"

Beth laughed. "I'm sure not a horsewoman, but I think I could manage that."

"Okay," Tor said. "Let's get started, then."

One by one they led the ponies over, and Tor and Samantha helped the children into the saddle, adjusted the stirrups, and showed them how to wrap their fingers in their pony's mane for support.

When all the children were mounted, Tor said to the others, "We'll start out walking the ponies around the ring. Follow me, and stay a couple of yards back from the pony in front of you. All set?" He looked at each of the children.

Samantha smiled at the children's wide-eyed expressions. Tor started forward, leading one of the wheelchair-bound little boys, Timmy, who was blond and blue eyed. Samantha followed, leading the black girl, whose name was Mandy Jarvis. She was absolutely adorable, with huge, thick-lashed dark eyes and a head of short black curls. Beth had told Samantha that the six-year-old had been involved in a serious accident the year before, when a car ran a stop sign and slammed into the Jarvis family car. There was a possibility that Mandy would recover full use of her legs, but it would take time and a lot of therapy.

Behind them Yvonne and Beth led two of the other wheelchair-bound students, Jane and Robert, both dark haired and a little nervous. Janet escorted Charmaine, who had a headful of strawberry blond curls. Last in the line was Gregg, leading Aaron, a beautiful child with angelic features but sadness in his dark eyes.

By the time they'd finished one circle of the ring, all the children were smiling with delight. Samantha heard Mandy's cheerful giggle. "I like this! I love horses, but I never rode one before. Can we go faster?"

"Not yet," Samantha said, laughing. "Maybe later."

Tor continued leading the line of ponies through more intricate figures. The children loved it. Then he explained some of the basics—how the reins worked and how to sit in the saddle, with shoulders back and head up. After thirty minutes Tor halted at the top of the ring and turned to the children. "Would you like to finish up with a trot?" he asked.

"Yes!" the children responded.

"All right. We'll trot straight down the center of the ring. Hold on tight. This is going to be a much bumpier ride." Tor looked over at Samantha and grinned, then called to the children, "Here we go!"

A chorus of giggles echoed in the ring as the six ponies trotted bouncily along. When they'd reached the other end of the ring, they all stopped and Tor asked, "So what did you think of your ride? Would you like to come again?"

The children vigorously nodded.

"Okay, we'll see what we can work out. We'll help you dismount now."

When the children were all back on the ground, Beth walked over to Tor and Samantha. "This was wonderful," she said. "To see the smiles on their faces is so rewarding. Would you be willing to do it again?"

"If you can arrange to get them here," Tor answered, "I'd be happy to put in an hour a week, or every other week. If Sammy, Yvonne, or Gregg can't be here, I can get some of my regular students to help. I'm sure they wouldn't mind."

"Well, I'd love to continue," Beth said. "What do you think, Janet?"

The other woman nodded. "I can't tell you how grateful I am. Could we arrange for a session every other week?"

"Fine," Tor said. "Wednesday afternoons?"

"It's a deal!" Janet said, extending her hand.

After the women and children had gone, Yvonne said to Samantha, "It makes you feel really good to see how happy those kids were."

"It also makes me feel pretty lucky," Gregg put in. "I don't know how I'd deal with being in a wheelchair."

"Neither do I," Samantha said, thinking how essential it was to have full use of her legs in her riding. What would she do if she couldn't ride?

"We'd better get these ponies put away," Tor said. "Sammy and I still have to go to Whitebrook and work Sierra."

They led the ponies out of the ring. With the light work they'd gotten, they didn't need to be cooled out. When the ponies were back in their stalls, Yvonne and Gregg waved Samantha and Tor off. "We're going to hang around here for a while and visit Cisco," Yvonne said. "See you in school tomorrow."

Tor and Samantha drove to Whitebrook and collected Sierra from his stall. As usual he showed his feisty nature and nearly pulled Samantha's arms out of their sockets in his eagerness to get outside.

Once Sierra was tacked up, they took him out to the inner turf course on the training oval. Samantha stood at the rail and watched as Tor put Sierra over a series of practice jumps. They weren't going to work Sierra hard, just keep him in top shape. They'd entered him in a steeplechase in mid-October, a week after Pride's race in the Gold Cup.

Tor and Sierra cantered the course, and Samantha admired as always their beauty and grace as they skimmed over the hedgelike fences. Then, coming off the second-to-last fence in the series, Sierra suddenly stumbled. Tor instantly pulled him up. It was unusual for Sierra to make a bad landing, since Tor timed their approaches and takeoffs so perfectly. Samantha waited for Tor to circle Sierra and put him back into a canter to approach the last fence. Instead she saw Tor dismount. She hurried toward them over the grass course.

"What's wrong?" she called as she reached them.

Tor was frowning and shaking his head. "We didn't land off that jump right. I think he may have pulled a shoulder muscle. His leg feels all right, but he's definitely uncomfortable." He led Sierra forward a few steps. The big colt moved awkwardly and was obviously in pain.

"It was my fault," Tor said unhappily. "I brought him in too close to the jump. Let's get him back to the barn and have Mike or your father take a look at him."

"Don't blame yourself," Samantha said, seeing Tor's troubled expression.

"I was in the saddle."

"It was an accident," Samantha told him as they slowly led Sierra back to the stable yard.

"I may have just ruined his chances of racing at Fair Hill, and I was really looking forward to it."

Samantha wished there were something she could say to cheer him up. Missing Fair Hill would be a disappointment, but she knew Tor was more concerned about the seriousness of Sierra's injury.

Her father was in the yard, and Samantha called to him, trying to keep any anxiety out of her voice. "Dad, would you take a look at Sierra? He took a misstep. He's favoring his right fore."

Mr. McLean hurried over. He knelt and carefully examined Sierra's foreleg. "No heat," he said. "His leg and ankle don't seem tender to my touch." He rose and gently examined Sierra's shoulder muscle with his fingers. The colt let out a distressed snort. "I'd say he's definitely pulled it—and pretty badly. I'd call the vet, though, and get a second opinion."

When Mike's vet arrived a half-hour later, they

had Sierra untacked and in his stall and had put a compress on his shoulder.

After a careful examination the vet confirmed Tor and Mr. McLean's diagnosis. "He's pulled his muscle all right, but it could be worse. I'll take some X rays of his leg just to be on the safe side. Continue with the compresses and give him a good massage. Light exercise when he's less uncomfortable."

"But we'll definitely have to pull him out of training?" Tor asked.

"For at least a couple of weeks," the vet replied. "You'll need to get the inflammation down before he puts any stress on that muscle."

Tor heaved a sigh and frowned. Samantha laid her hand on his arm. They both had big dreams for Sierra's future, and competing in the Fair Hill 'chase would have brought Sierra that much closer to getting into the top ranks. "Don't blame yourself," Samantha told Tor. "It's a setback, but he's going to be all right—and there's next spring to look forward to."

Tor nodded. "I know. Disappointments are part of racing and showing horses. But I can't help feeling bad about it." He looked over at Samantha and gave a weak smile.

"So, monster," Samantha said to Sierra, "looks like you're going to have a longer rest than we expected." She cautiously rubbed the colt's nose, but Sierra wasn't in a biting mood. He just gave a distressed whicker.

"Don't worry, boy, we'll fix you up," she said.

She and Tor stayed with Sierra for another hour,

giving the colt a long massage. Len had taught her the technique, and Sierra huffed with relief as her strong fingers relaxed the tension in his muscles. Tor wanted to stay longer, but he had an evening college class and had to drive back to Lexington. He kissed her good-bye. "I'll see you tomorrow," he said. "I'll pick you up after school and take you over for your driving test."

Samantha felt her stomach lurch at being reminded of the test. She and Tor had gone out for several practice sessions, but she still couldn't help feeling nervous.

"Don't worry," Tor said. "You'll do fine." Then he rubbed his finger along her cheek. "And thanks for trying to cheer me up about Sierra."

"Anytime," she said with a smile.

Samantha's hands were cold and clammy the next afternoon as she got into the car with the driving inspector. She tried to clear her thoughts and not think about the mistakes she could make. She listened carefully to the inspector's instructions as he directed her through the Lexington streets. Her heart was pounding by the time she pulled back into the motor vehicle lot, but she thought she'd done okay. She'd even done a perfect job of parallel parking—not like last time, when it had taken her three tries.

Still, she held her breath as she looked over to the inspector and waited for his decision. He nodded and smiled. "You passed. Congratulations. Take these forms and go into the office to get your license."

"Thank you!" Samantha blurted. She had to force herself not to hug the inspector. Finally she was getting her license!

When she told Tor the good news, he gave her a big smacking kiss on the lips. "I told you you'd do fine," he said with a grin. "Why don't you drive us home?"

Samantha gave Pride a final half-mile breeze on the following Tuesday, the day before he would be flown up to the Belmont track in New York for the Jockey Club Gold Cup. Ashleigh watched from the rail with stopwatch in hand. Pride did everything perfectly, breezing out the half-mile effortlessly. Samantha leaned down and hugged his neck before she rode off the track. "You're something, big guy! I think you've just made Ashleigh really happy with that work—and me too!"

Pride whuffed in gratitude for the praise.

Ashleigh was smiling from ear to ear as Samantha rode up.

"He's set!" she said. "Great work, Sammy. I've still got a case of the jitters, though, with him racing against Lord Ainsley again."

"Pride's beaten him before," Samantha reminded her. "And Pride's going to be the fresher horse."

"I wasn't doubting Pride," Ashleigh said quickly. "I'm just dreading the tension I know is going to be in the air. Lavinia and Brad aren't going to make the prerace atmosphere fun for me."

Mike walked up as Samantha dismounted. "I just

had a call from Ken Maddock," he said. "It's good news for you, Ash. Maddock has convinced Brad to pull Lord Ainsley out of the Gold Cup. He said the colt just hasn't bounced back the way he should, and he'd rather rest him and have him fresh for the Breeders' Cup, which is by far the more important race."

"Whoa!" said Samantha, smiling. "I wonder what Lavinia had to say."

Mike chuckled. "Maddock tried to be discreet, but I got the impression she raised one heck of a stink."

"Figures," Ashleigh said wryly. "Lavinia wouldn't stop to think of the horse's welfare."

Samantha felt like a load had been taken off her shoulders as she walked Pride around the yard to cool him out. "I know you could have beaten him," she said to Pride, "but it's going to be a much easier race for you with Lord Ainsley out. You'll win it!"

Pride threw up his elegant head and whinnied loudly.

Samantha laughed. "Right!"

6

SAMANTHA FLEW UP TO NEW YORK ON FRIDAY AFTERNOON
to join Ashleigh, Mike, and Pride at the Belmont track.
She was feeling confident and hopeful. Pride looked
wonderful, and with Lord Ainsley out of the race
Samantha didn't think they had anything to worry
about. She was upset to see, though, as she gave Pride
a final meticulous grooming before the race, that
Ashleigh was growing increasingly pensive as race
time approached. She paced outside Pride's stall, mut-
tering to herself as she went through a mental check-
list. Jilly Gordon, Pride's regular jockey, had come in
for the ride and was already in the jockeys' quarters.
Samantha hadn't seen Brad or Lavinia, which surprised her. Even though Lord Ainsley had been
scratched, she would have expected them to be on
hand to accept the honors for Townsend Acres if Pride
won. They rarely missed the chance for free publicity.

"Relax," Mike finally told Ashleigh, putting his

arm around her shoulders and making her sit down on the bench outside Pride's stall. "You've done everything just right, and with Lord Ainsley out of the race Pride should have an easy time of it. His only challenge might come from that foreign horse, Regency, but he hasn't raced much in this country."

"It's not that," Ashleigh said. "Did you see the *Daily Racing Form* today?" Ashleigh picked the paper up off the bench and quoted, "'. . . Although Wonder's Pride put in an outstanding performance in the Whitney Handicap, there are questions whether Ashleigh Griffen has the experience as trainer to keep the big horse at his peak. She'll have a difficult task filling the shoes of Charlie Burke. Further questions have been raised as to why Wonder's Pride wasn't put in the hands of Townsend Acres' trainer, Ken Maddock, after Burke's death in July.'" Ashleigh made a growling noise.

"You know who probably started the rumor," Samantha said, finishing up with Pride and closing his stall door behind her.

"And the *Racing Form* is still backing Pride as favorite."

"Yeah, because the rest of the field is so mediocre."

"Come on, Ash," Mike said. "You know Maddock agreed that Pride was better off with you training him. Don't let some stupid comment in the paper get to you."

"I know I shouldn't. I should be thankful and relieved that Brad and Lavinia aren't here hassling us. I'm sorry," Ashleigh said. "My mood will be getting to the rest of you. I'll snap out of it, I promise." Ashleigh checked her watch. "It's time to take him to the receiving barn. Sammy, is he all set to go?"

"All ready. He's looking gorgeous as usual."

At that Ashleigh smiled. "Okay, let's take him out."

Samantha led Pride out of his stall. His gleaming copper coat was covered by the green-and-gold satin Townsend Acres sheet. His head was high and his ears pricked alertly. As usual, Samantha's heart swelled. Pride looked like a champion.

There was no sign of Lavinia or Brad at the saddling paddock or walking ring either, for which Samantha was thankful. Ashleigh had her mind totally on business now as she gave Jilly a leg into the saddle.

"You don't need instructions from me," Ashleigh told the blond jockey. "You've ridden him before and know how he likes to run. Just keep your eye on the six horse, Regency. He could be a surprise. Good luck!"

Jilly gathered the reins and smiled. "We'll go out there and show them our heels. Won't we, Pride?"

Pride gave a quick snort as Samantha led him and Jilly once more around the ring before the field went out to the track. The crowd certainly appreciated Pride. They smiled and cheered as Samantha led him past. When it was time for the horses to file out to the track, Samantha dropped a kiss on Pride's nose. "I know you're going to go out there and do a fantastic job. I love you."

Then Samantha, Ashleigh, and Mike hurried up to the stands to watch the race.

As Samantha had expected, Jilly got Pride out of the gate quickly and settled him just off the flank of the early speed horse, Costar, who was setting fairly brisk fractions. Samantha knew from his past form that the speed horse probably wouldn't be able to sustain the pace for the full mile and a quarter. Pride was in perfect striking position. Jilly sat patiently in the saddle, biding her time until the end of the backstretch.

As the field headed into the far turn, Jilly gave Pride rein. He instantly accelerated and effortlessly passed the lead horse, who indeed was tiring.

Samantha scanned her binoculars over the field, looking for the foreign horse. She knew he was a late closer, but he had only run on American tracks twice before. She didn't think he had it in him to catch Pride. To her dismay, she saw that Regency was making a very big move around the far turn, passing horses on the outside.

Her breath caught. "Do you see that?" she said to Ashleigh.

"Yes, but I'm not worried yet. You know Pride's going to go into another gear when he changes leads in the stretch."

Regency was now up into second, three lengths behind Pride and gaining. Jilly glanced back under her arm and saw him coming. As they came out of the far turn Regency was up on Pride's flank, and his strides were eating up the ground.

Samantha's heart was in her throat. She knew

Pride had more in reserve, but Regency was coming on so fast. What if Pride didn't accelerate soon enough? At the top of the stretch Pride changed leads. Jilly kneaded her hands up his neck, encouraging him, and Pride shot forward. Regency's jockey had gone to his whip, but Pride powered away from the other horse.

The crowds in the stands were on their feet screaming encouragement to Pride, roaring approval as Pride and Jilly flashed under the wire the definitive winners. Pride's performance had been effortless.

In the winner's circle the television commentator hurried over to interview Ashleigh. Of course his first question centered around the Breeders' Cup and a matchup with Lord Ainsley.

"First of all," Ashleigh responded, "Pride and Lord Ainsley won't be the only horses running in the Classic. Anything can happen in a horse race, but Pride always gives his best."

"There's been some speculation that you weren't ready to fill Charlie Burke's shoes," the commentator added. "I guess you've shown otherwise today."

Ashleigh smiled. "I hope so, but there always will be doubters. We'll just keep doing our best and trying to prove them wrong."

Samantha gave her friend a subtle thumbs-up, imagining Lavinia and Brad's reactions to Pride's win. She chuckled to herself.

"At this point," the commentator continued, "you must be giving thought to Horse of the Year honors."

"It would be nice," Ashleigh said, "but we're not

in this business simply for the glory. We're in it for love of the sport."

With only a little over two weeks to the Breeders' Cup, Samantha tried not to think of the pressure they would all be under, Pride included. The racing reporters were already building up the match between Pride and Lord Ainsley, almost totally disregarding the other ten entrants in the Classic field. The frenzy would only increase as Breeders' Cup day approached.

Samantha was up at dawn every morning so that she and Ashleigh could work Pride. He continued in perfect form, moving smoothly through his gallops, accelerating rapidly when Samantha asked him to breeze. After school Samantha spent more hours with the big horse, giving him a daily massage and meticulous grooming, keeping him relaxed and happy. The Classic was such an important race. Samantha wanted to ensure that Pride was at his physical and mental best going into it. She and Len were also giving Sierra a daily massage and dose of TLC, and the colt was improving.

Samantha wasn't the only one doting on Pride. Ashleigh and Len made frequent visits to his stall, and Sidney the cat was his near-constant companion.

Sidney's parents, Snowshoe and Jeeves, had produced another litter, and Sidney was definitely miffed at the attention the two new arrivals were receiving. He aloofly ignored his younger siblings and spent more time than ever at Pride's stall.

That Saturday, Ashleigh asked Samantha to ride

over to Townsend Acres with her when she made her weekly visit to see Townsend Princess. Although Wonder's second foal would be trained at Townsend Acres, Ashleigh was still Princess's co-owner and felt a special attachment to the filly.

Samantha eagerly agreed, but felt uneasy. "What if we run into Brad or Lavinia?"

Ashleigh shrugged. "Let's hope we don't, but I have every right to visit Princess. Lavinia and Brad sure don't think twice about barging in over here to see Mr. Wonderful."

Samantha knew that was true. Too often Brad and Lavinia had shown up unannounced at Whitebrook to take a proprietary look at the foal.

Samantha felt strange as Ashleigh headed up the long Townsend Acres drive, past the breeding manager's house and the breeding barns, past white-fenced paddocks to the training area. This had been her home for two years. Everything was so familiar, and she was hit with a rush of memories, good and bad. There were the good memories of helping Ashleigh train Fleet Goddess and Pride. And there were the bad memories of the problems Brad had caused her father, which had prompted him to leave and go to Whitebrook to work. She had been devastated at the move then, but now she couldn't be happier that they had left Townsend Acres.

Ashleigh parked in the drive by the yearling barn. Townsend Acres was a much larger operation than Whitebrook, with three times as many horses in training and a live-in staff of six. As they approached the yearling barn they saw Hank and another groom working two yearlings on a longe line in the circular training enclosure behind the stable building.

They walked up to the ring to watch. To Samantha's dismay, she saw Lavinia was already there, standing with her back toward them, her hands on her hips.

"There's Princess," Ashleigh said, ignoring Lavinia and pointing to the chestnut filly that was circling Hank at a trot at the end of the longe line.

"She's grown into a real beauty, hasn't she?" Samantha said quietly. "She looks like Wonder." She studied Princess, who had the same bright chestnut coat and white blaze as her dam. The filly's neck was arched gracefully, and she moved with a sure, energetic gait.

Hank circled the filly twice more. Lavinia walked farther around the ring, then her haughty voice cut the air. "Can't you speed things up a little?" she said to Hank. "She's not making enough progress. You're repeating the same exercise day after day—walk, trot, canter. By now she should have a rider in the saddle."

"I've trained hundreds of yearlings," Hank said tersely. "This is the way it's done. You're laying a foundation here. You don't rush things and move ahead until the horse is fully confident about what it's already learned."

"But she knows this!" Lavinia snapped.

Hank glowered back at her. "Tomorrow I'll start her with a rider." He glanced up and saw Ashleigh and Samantha at the other side of the ring. He smiled.

Lavinia followed his gaze. Her face tightened when she saw the two young women. "What are you doing here?" she demanded of Ashleigh.

"I'm checking on my filly," Ashleigh said calmly. "I like to see how the training is coming along, and I think Hank is doing a great job."

Lavinia narrowed her eyes angrily, but she knew Ashleigh had every right to watch Princess's training session and certainly more right, as half-owner, to make any comments or suggestions to Hank.

"If I were you," Lavinia snapped, "I would be spending time with the horse you *are* training— before he's *retired*." She gave Ashleigh a snide little smile, then sauntered away from the ring.

"She never lets up, does she?" Ashleigh said to Samantha.

"She only made that comment about Pride being retired to upset you."

"Oh, I know," Ashleigh replied.

Hank was frowning as he led Princess from the ring and joined Ashleigh and Samantha.

"Is she down here every day?" Ashleigh asked him.

Hank nodded unhappily. "Near enough. She and Brad are both taking a real interest in the filly. There's talk that Brad wants to handle her training himself."

"No!" Ashleigh exclaimed. "What does Maddock have to say about that?"

"What *can* he say?" Hank responded. "Brad's in charge of the decision making until Clay Townsend gets back from England. Of course, the filly won't be getting any intensive training until early next year.

What bothers me," Hank added, "is that Brad has been coaching Lavinia on her riding, and she's planning on being one of the regular exercise riders."

"The way she rides?" Ashleigh cried. "Brad has to be out of his mind! Even with coaching, she's got no feel for horses. She is totally insensitive and has no idea what makes them tick. She'd just better stay away from Princess!"

"Brad's not a fool," Hank told her. "He's got too many hopes for the filly. He's not going to put up an inexperienced rider—even if the rider is his wife."

"But we all know how Lavinia twists Brad around her little finger," Samantha said with disgust. "She always seems to get what she wants—except when it comes to Pride."

"From what I've heard," Hank said, "it's her money that's backing Townsend Acres' breeding expansion in England. And she's already pouring money into the operation here."

Ashleigh frowned. "So she expects to have some say about how things are done. That's what worries me."

"I know how you both feel," Hank said, "but remember what Charlie used to say—it's no use worrying about a problem before it happens. He was right."

"Even so," Ashleigh said. "If she dares to get in Princess's saddle, even once, she'll hear from me—loud and clear!"

7

SAMANTHA STOOD IN THE DRIVE OUTSIDE TOR'S STABLE ON Friday afternoon as he, Yvonne, and Gregg prepared to head out for the show in Virginia. It was the last weekend in October and growing chilly. "I'll be thinking about you," Samantha said, "but you're both going to do great. I know it!"

Yvonne's lips flickered in a nervous smile. "I hope!"

"You will," Samantha said firmly. "I only wish I could be there to see you."

"You just concentrate on getting Pride ready for the race next weekend," Tor said, putting his arm around Samantha's shoulders and giving them a squeeze. "I'll call you tonight after we get there."

Tor's father stepped around the big horse van. Yvonne's mount, Cisco, Tor's white Thoroughbred gelding, Top Hat, and one of Mr. Nelson's hunters were already stalled inside. Mr. Nelson would be competing in one of the hunter divisions at the Virginia show. "The horses are set," he called. "Everybody ready?"

"Ready as we can be," Tor replied.

"Have a safe trip, and I'll talk to you tonight," Samantha said as Tor kissed her cheek. She really wished she could be at the show to watch him and Top Hat compete. The expression in Tor's blue eyes told her he wished the same, but understood that Pride was her priority now.

Samantha turned to give Yvonne a hug. "Good luck, kiddo!"

"Thanks!"

Yvonne needed the boost to her confidence that would come from competing in a big out-of-state show. For Tor and Top Hat, a ribbon in their advanced-jumping event would be a step toward entering the National Horse Show in February. Samantha watched wistfully as they all climbed into the oversized cab of the van. Tor started the engine, and Samantha waved and blew them all kisses as the van rolled off down the drive. When they were out of sight, she turned and walked toward her father's car. Today was the first time she'd taken it on her own since she'd gotten her license, and she was a little bit nervous. She stayed well within the speed limit as she left Lexington, then followed the country roads home to Whitebrook.

It was late afternoon when Samantha parked the car in front of the McLean cottage. The sun was already sinking behind the rolling hills. With the days getting shorter, more chores had to be crammed into what daylight hours there were. Before going into the barn to check on Pride, Samantha stopped at the mares' paddock. Len and Vic had brought in the weanlings and some of the mares. Wonder was still in the paddock, growing slightly round with the foal she was due to deliver in March. She came to the rail when she saw Samantha and sniffed Samantha's jacket pocket, looking for a carrot.

"Sorry, girl," Samantha said, rubbing Wonder's ears, "I don't have any with me. I'll give you a treat when you're back in your stall." Wonder huffed out a soft breath, obviously enjoying having her ears scratched. Samantha continued speaking softly. "There's a big weekend coming up. Your son's racing in the Breeders' Cup, and if he wins, there's a good chance he'll be named Horse of the Year. How do you like that?" Wonder nickered. "Pretty good, huh? But I think all your foals inherited your winning genes, including the little one growing in there." Samantha ran a gentle hand down Wonder's side. As she did, Len walked up with Wonder's lead shank and smiled at Samantha.

"I guess you're getting excited about next weekend," he said. "Pride looked real good to me when I watched you work him this morning."

"He's on his toes," Samantha agreed, "but it's not going to be an easy race."

"No, but he's had tough races before and has always shown his stuff. Charlie would be proud of the job Ashleigh and you are doing with him."

Samantha smiled. She thought of Charlie all the time when they were working Pride, imagining what the old trainer's reactions would be were he still alive. "I know Ashleigh's nervous, though," she said.

"I don't suppose she'd be normal if she wasn't a little anxious," Len replied. "But Pride couldn't be in better shape. We'll just have to give her all the support we can."

Wonder had seen the lead shank and whickered with a touch of impatience.

"You ready to go in for your dinner, pretty lady?" Len asked. He opened the gate and clipped the lead to Wonder's halter. The mare eagerly stepped out of the paddock.

"I'll walk back with you," Samantha said. "I promised her a carrot. Then I've got to check on Pride and Sierra."

"Looks like Sierra's feeling better," Len remarked. "He was ready to take a nip out of me this morning when I didn't get his feed bucket hung fast enough. But he's a tough one." The black man smiled. Len was one of Sierra's biggest fans.

The barn was warm and hay scented. The mares that were already in their stalls nickered and stomped as they awaited their dinners. As Len put Wonder into her roomy box, Samantha went to the tack room to get a carrot. She broke it into pieces and fed Wonder. The mare chomped gratefully. Samantha gave Wonder a last pat and headed out to the training barn.

Entering the training barn, Samantha saw Ashleigh standing outside Pride's stall. She was leaning on the half-door and frowning thoughtfully. As usual, Sidney sat on top of the stall partition and was busily grooming himself. "Hi!" Samantha called.

Ashleigh jumped and turned her head.

"Sorry, I didn't mean to startle you," Samantha said.

"I was just thinking." Ashleigh lifted a rolled newspaper and handed it to Samantha. "Have you seen this? The lead article."

Samantha unfolded the paper to see the sports section of that day's *Lexington Herald*. A TWO-HORSE RACE IN THE CLASSIC, the headline read. The Breeders' Cup was causing even more than the usual excitement locally since the races would be run in Kentucky that year. Samantha skimmed the article, not finding anything strange, then her eye caught on one line. "According to Townsend Acres, co-owners of Wonder's Pride, the Classic may be the Derby winner's last race. Regardless of how he fares in the Classic, he may be retired immediately after the race to begin his stud career in the spring. According to Brad Townsend, 'He is a valuable stallion and it wouldn't be wise to risk injury by racing him another year.' Ashleigh Griffen, Wonder's Pride's trainer and co-owner, could not be reached for comment."

Samantha looked up from the paper. "Ash, this

can't be for real. It's got to be Brad making things up. Mr. Townsend hasn't said a word about retiring Pride, and there is absolutely no reason why Pride can't race at least another year. A lot of stallions aren't retired until they're five or six."

"Mr. Townsend hasn't said anything yet, but he's been in England, don't forget."

"So Brad figures he can get away with starting a rumor like this, knowing it will upset you," Samantha reasoned. "Mr. Townsend will be back next weekend. You can straighten it out." She paused when she saw the expression on Ashleigh's face. "What's wrong? You don't think there's any truth to this. Mr. Townsend wouldn't do anything without talking to you."

Ashleigh sighed. "I don't know why, but I have an awful feeling that this time there's some truth behind what Brad said."

"Why do you think that?" Samantha asked anxiously. "I know Brad and Lavinia have both wanted to see Pride retired so he wouldn't be competing against Lord Ainsley, but why should you think there's any truth to it this time?"

"I don't know. I just have this feeling," Ashleigh said. "Remember how distracted Mr. Townsend was when he was here last? He's so wrapped up in starting this breeding operation in England, I think he's losing interest in what's going on here. I think he could be convinced that it's time Pride was retired."

"You don't know that," Samantha said quickly.

"Why couldn't the reporter who wrote the article reach you for comment?"

"He left a message on Mike's machine," Ashleigh said, "but I didn't call him back. I've had too much to do, and Charlie never bothered with reporters before a big race. I didn't know the reporter was calling about this retirement rumor."

"Why don't you call the paper now, Ash, and straighten it out?" Samantha suggested. "And then just ignore anything else Brad or Lavinia has to say."

"I intend to," Ashleigh said. But Samantha didn't like the look on Ashleigh's face as she strode away. Was there something Ashleigh wasn't telling her?

Tor called on Saturday night just as Samantha, her father, and Beth were finishing dinner.

She was thrilled to hear his voice. "So how did it go?" she asked eagerly.

"It couldn't have gone better," Tor replied. "Yvonne and Cisco got a first in Intermediate, and it was a tough course. No one got a clean round, but they did best with two faults."

"All right! And how did you and Top Hat do?" Samantha saw her father and Beth looking over with interest.

"We didn't get the blue. We came in second, but with only a couple of faults. After being out of serious competition all summer, that's a good start. I'm happy. We can only improve off today's show."

"Was the course difficult?" Samantha asked with concern.

"It was a bummer, but I'm definitely happy."

"Good. So am I! Is Yvonne there? Let me talk to her a second."

Yvonne was bubbly and excited when she got on the phone and Samantha congratulated her. "I told you you would do well," Samantha said.

"Right! It doesn't seem bad now looking back, but I sure didn't feel that way entering the ring."

Samantha and Tor talked a few minutes longer. "We'll be back tomorrow afternoon about three," Tor said. "Can you meet us at the stable? I thought we could all go into town and celebrate."

"I'll be there!"

She was smiling broadly when she hung up the phone. "So, I guess it was a good weekend for them," her father said.

"It was." Samantha gave her father and Beth all the details.

"I meant to ask you," her father said after a moment. "I saw the article in the paper yesterday about Pride's supposed retirement. Did Ashleigh see it?"

"Yes, and she was pretty upset."

"I hope she doesn't take it too much to heart," Mr. McLean said. "I can't believe Clay Townsend is seriously considering retiring Pride after this season. This sounds like more of Brad's troublemaking."

"I thought the same thing," Samantha agreed. "But Ashleigh thought there might be some truth in it. She

76

said Mr. Townsend seems to be losing interest in the Lexington operation."

Her father frowned. "Let's hope not. Anyway, he'll be back for the Breeders' Cup. Ashleigh can sort it out with him face to face then."

"Yes," Samantha said, becoming concerned now, too.

8

ASHLEIGH HAD CALLED THE REPORTER AT THE *LEXINGTON Herald* and told him that the rumor about Pride's retirement had been just that—a rumor. She'd also called Brad and had angrily asked him what he thought he was up to. "They misquoted me," Brad had glibly told Ashleigh. "All I said was that retirement was one option."

"Sure," Ashleigh told Samantha. "Does he really expect me to believe that?" Unfortunately the rumor had already taken root. Calls poured in from people asking about Pride's imminent retirement. By Tuesday morning, as they prepared to leave for Churchill Downs, Ashleigh was ready to pull out her hair.

"We'll take care of any calls that come in," Samantha told Ashleigh as they finished loading Pride and Blues King into the van. Mike had decided to enter Blues King in the Breeders' Cup Sprint.

"It's just so annoying and unnecessary," Ashleigh

said. "Anyway, thanks, Sammy. I'll see you on Wednesday night."

"I can't wait!"

Ashleigh, Mike, and Len would go over to Louisville in the van. Samantha was taking Thursday and Friday off from school and would go over with her father on Wednesday night. Tor, Yvonne, Gregg, and Beth would drive over on Friday afternoon.

At school on Wednesday, Samantha was surprised at how many classmates came up to wish her and Pride good luck.

"I don't know why you're surprised," Yvonne told her with a grin. "Everybody knows all about Pride from your articles. Of course they're hoping he'll win." Samantha's tribute to Charlie had come out in the October issue of the paper, and she was centering her next article around the Breeders' Cup.

"But I hardly know some of the kids who wished us luck. And I'm sure a lot of them usually have no interest in horse racing."

"Pride's famous—and everyone at school knows you're his groom. You've even been on television. It's exciting! If Pride wins, it'll be like one of us winning."

When Samantha and her father arrived in Louisville that night, the streets were still filled with traffic. Although it was the first week in November, with temperatures only in the thirties, the city was bustling. It was almost as hectic as Derby week. Fortunately Ashleigh had booked them all into a motel near the track months before.

"We'll go to the track first," Mr. McLean said. "I

imagine you can't wait to see Pride. And I'd like to see how Blues King is doing."

Len was outside Pride's stall when Samantha and her father reached the Townsend Acres stabling. "So you made it," he called. "Ashleigh and Mike have already headed to their room. Pride's all set for the night. I just checked him, but I guess you'll want to peek in and say hello. He'll be glad to see you."

Samantha was already headed toward the stall. She unlatched the top half-door and peered in. Pride had been dozing, but he whickered happily when he saw her and stepped over to the door. Samantha took his head and dropped a kiss on his velvet nose. "I won't keep you up, boy. I just wanted to let you know I was here."

Behind her, she heard her father and Len talking. "Lord Ainsley's only a few stalls down," Len was saying. "Ashleigh's not too happy about that, but what can you do? Townsend Acres has only these two running in the Breeders' Cup, so they haven't reserved a lot of stalls."

Samantha turned. "Have Brad and Lavinia been around?" she asked.

"I saw Brad yesterday," Len said, "but I think he only stopped by to talk to Maddock. It's been quiet, if you don't count all the reporters and sightseers trying to get a look at Pride and Lord Ainsley. The way some of them are gawking, you'd think there was only one race being run Saturday and only two horses in it."

"But Pride seems calm," Samantha said.

"I've been making sure no one bothered him," Len

told her. "That hasn't always been easy."

"I can imagine." Samantha had been to enough big races with Pride to know that some people could get very pushy and obnoxious.

"Well, let me take a look at Blues King," Mr. McLean said, "then I think we'd better get some sleep. It's going to be a busy day tomorrow."

Samantha nodded and gave Pride a last kiss. "See you in the morning," she said, closing the top door of the stall and bolting it. She gave a parting wave to Len, then followed her father down the shedrow to Blues King's stall.

Samantha's alarm went off at four thirty. As she reached for it in the darkness, she was instantly awake and filled with anticipation for the day ahead. That morning she would be giving Pride his last work before the Classic. She loved riding workouts at a racecourse—pounding over the dirt in the early light, past empty stands that in a few hours would be overflowing; watching other horses and riders work; feeling the anticipation and excitement that always built before a big race.

An hour later when Ashleigh, Samantha, and Mike approached the track with Pride, Samantha saw that quite a crowd had gathered to watch that morning's workouts. She also saw Brad and Lavinia standing with Ken Maddock, who was holding Lord Ainsley. Brad was dressed for riding, which meant he would probably be working Lord Ainsley himself.

Pride snorted excitedly as Ashleigh gave

Samantha a leg into the saddle. He was ready and eager to get out on the track. Jilly and her jockey husband, Craig Avery, walked over as Ashleigh gave Samantha instructions. "Gallop him through three quarters, Sammy, then breeze out the last quarter. He knows this track. I just want to sharpen him up."

"Gotcha," Samantha said, gathering the reins.

"I understand Lord Ainsley's never raced at Churchill Downs," Jilly said to Ashleigh.

"No, he hasn't."

"That could be to our advantage," Jilly said. "Not every horse likes the surface here."

"I've been wondering about that," Ashleigh agreed. "Maddock gave him a couple of works earlier in the week. They weren't very impressive, but I don't think Maddock was trying to push him."

"It'll be interesting to see how he goes today," Jilly said. "It looks like Brad's going to be riding."

Brad had yet to get in the saddle. He and Maddock were still talking, which was fine with Samantha. She didn't really want to be working at the same time as Brad and Lord Ainsley.

"Okay," Ashleigh said, patting Pride's shoulder. "Take him out."

Samantha tapped Pride with her heels and moved him forward through the gap and onto the track. Half a dozen other horses were already working. It would be a busy morning with the Breeders' Cup only two days away.

Pride's strides were smooth and relaxed as Samantha warmed him up at a trot and then a canter along the outside rail. When they'd lapped the track once, Samantha checked for other horses, then tightened her left rein and moved Pride in close to the inside rail. She gave him rein, and Pride instantly strode out in a slow but ground-eating gallop. They pounded around the course.

As they neared the quarter pole Samantha crouched lower over Pride's neck. He knew what was coming, and when Samantha clucked and kneaded her hands up his neck, Pride changed leads and burst into a breezing gallop. They were flying! Pride's mane whipped back into Samantha's face, and she lost herself to the sounds of his rhythmically pounding hooves and snorted breaths. They came off the turn and powered down the stretch. From the corner of her eye, Samantha saw the rail posts flashing by. Their time was excellent. She didn't need a stopwatch to know that. As they swept under the wire Samantha stood in her stirrups and gradually pulled Pride up.

"That's the way!" she told him breathlessly. "Perfect!" Pride's neck was arched as Samantha turned him to head back to the gap. She saw Brad and Lord Ainsley coming onto the track. They jogged past in the opposite direction, but Brad never looked Samantha's way.

Ashleigh was all smiles as Samantha rode up. "Nice," Ashleigh told Samantha. "Very nice. I couldn't have asked for more!"

Samantha grinned and rubbed her hand over Pride's neck.

"That work should guarantee him going in as the favorite Saturday," Craig said.

Pride's workout had definitely caught the attention of the crowd that had gathered to watch. Samantha continued to smile as she dismounted and pulled up the stirrups, again praising Pride as Ashleigh checked him over. Len walked over with a grin to collect the big horse and take him to the barn. "That was a pleasure to see," he told Samantha. "You go ahead and watch the competition work. I'll start cooling him."

"Thanks, Len. I do want to see Lord Ainsley's workout." Samantha walked to the rail with the others.

It was pretty obvious when Brad set Lord Ainsley down to gallop that the bay horse wasn't handling the track surface as well as he might. He was trying, but he wasn't digging in the way Samantha had seen him dig in in the past. His strides almost seemed labored. Brad didn't look happy when he pulled Lord Ainsley up and rode off the track.

"You didn't need a stopwatch to see those fractions were slow," Jilly said. "He didn't seem to be handling the surface, but that's good news for us."

"Yes," Ashleigh said, "though that doesn't mean he'll run a bad race Saturday. Today could have been a fluke."

"I don't know," Jilly said. "Maddock sure looks disappointed."

Samantha watched as Brad dismounted. She sympathized with Maddock. She knew how she'd feel if Pride had put in as lackluster a workout.

"I've learned the hard way never to underestimate Brad," Ashleigh said. "And with LeBlanc riding, they can be dangerous. LeBlanc's an ace when it comes to strategy."

Still, for the rest of the day Ashleigh seemed much more cheerful and relaxed, not that any of them could truly relax with the Breeders' Cup two days away. Ashleigh was barraged by reporters wanting to know her reactions to that morning's workouts. And the following morning's papers had Pride as the clear favorite. The mood a few stalls down was much less cheerful. Ken Maddock had taken Lord Ainsley out on the track himself earlier that morning to see how he was handling the surface.

"You have to feel for him," Len told Samantha.

"Oh, I do."

Later that morning, though, when post positions for the Classic were drawn, Lavinia and Brad arrived at Lord Ainsley's stall wreathed in smiles. When Ashleigh and Mike arrived a few minutes later, they weren't smiling.

"You won't believe this," Ashleigh said unhappily. "A fourteen-horse field, and what do we draw—the very *outside* post! He won't even be in the main gate. He'll be in the auxiliary gate!"

It wasn't good news at all, especially considering Pride's running style. "What did Lord Ainsley draw?" Samantha asked.

"The four spot. Perfect for him. It might be enough to balance out his dislike for the surface."

Samantha knew Brad and Lavinia couldn't have had

anything to do with the outcome of the draw. It was just bad luck for Ashleigh and Pride—very bad luck.

"You know how this is going to affect our strategy," Ashleigh said to Jilly.

Jilly nodded. "I'll have to get him out incredibly fast and sprint around most of the field if we're going to get up near the lead. He'll have to cover a lot of ground, and that's going to use up a lot of steam so early in the race. I could try running him off the pace."

Ashleigh shook her head. "He'd hate it and only get frustrated. That would take even more out of him."

"So I'll shoot for getting him up near the early lead."

"There are several horses that aren't going to make it easy," Ashleigh said. "And all of them have the advantage of better post positions. Lord Ainsley will be up there if he runs to past form. The two European horses have early speed, and so does Costar."

Jilly scowled. "That outside post sure puts a glitch in things, but I think Pride can do it—if everything else goes all right."

"Nothing's ever easy," Mike said. "At least Blues King drew a decent post position."

As the news of the draw spread, a steady stream of press people filed through the backside. Pride's post position was obviously affecting his odds as favorite. Samantha didn't care so much about that, but she knew that Pride was going to have a very difficult race ahead of him.

When Tor, Yvonne, and Gregg arrived late that

afternoon, Samantha greeted them eagerly. She told them all the news as they went to see Pride.

"Brilliant horses like Pride have overcome poor post positions to win," Tor said to Samantha after she'd told them about that morning's draw.

"But it's not going to be easy, and I hate to see things made tougher for him than they have to be. Ashleigh was walking on clouds after his workout yesterday, especially when Lord Ainsley didn't work well at all."

"If Pride doesn't win tomorrow," Yvonne asked, "does that mean he's out of the running for Horse of the Year?"

"Not necessarily. He'd only be out of the running if Lord Ainsley wins."

"Why don't we all take a walk into town and get something to eat?" Tor suggested. "Len's here to keep an eye on Pride."

Samantha nodded. "Good idea. I'm ready for a break. I'll warn you, though, Louisville's a mob scene."

"I noticed when we drove in," Tor said.

They had to wait nearly an hour to get seated in a Mexican restaurant, but the food was great, and over their meal Samantha told them about the horses running in the Classic and about the favorites for the other six Breeders' Cup races.

The night air was chilly as they left the restaurant and walked back to the barns. Samantha wasn't surprised to find that Ashleigh and Mike were still on the backside. People were gathered outside Lord Ainsley's stall, too. Brad and Lavinia obviously were celebrating Lord Ainsley's post position.

Samantha was surprised a few minutes later to see Brad break away from the group and head in Ashleigh's direction. Brad had avoided them until now, and Samantha wondered uneasily what was up.

"I just heard from my father," Brad said to Ashleigh. "He'll be here first thing in the morning. A real shame about Pride's post position," he added with total insincerity. "It really would be a miracle if he can overcome the disadvantage to win."

"Miracles have been known to happen," Ashleigh said coldly. "But I don't think we'll need one."

Brad smiled. "Well, if you don't mind facing the embarrassment of having Pride finish off the board . . ." He shrugged. "If it were me, I would consider scratching him. I think my father might agree, and people would understand, considering his post position."

"Stuff it, Brad. I'm not interested in your opinions, and I have no intention of scratching. I know your father will agree with me when I talk to him in the morning."

Brad gave another of his two-faced smiles. "Suit yourself. It's your funeral."

"He's awful cheerful for someone whose horse doesn't like the track," Samantha said angrily as Brad walked off.

"Maddock got a better workout out of Lord Ainsley this morning," Mike said. "And the track's been showing a bias that could work in Lord Ainsley's favor. The surface is faster and less deep along the rail."

"Oh," Samantha said glumly. That really could work in Lord Ainsley's favor if his jockey could keep him in close to the rail on the firmer ground. Then again, there was no guarantee LeBlanc could do that. But it was definitely turning into a much tougher race for Pride than she'd anticipated.

9

THE NEXT MORNING WENT BY IN A BLUR. THE BACKSIDE was absolutely crazy, although Samantha did her best to keep Pride calm and shielded from the worst of the commotion. Yvonne and Gregg toured the barn area, while Tor stayed with Samantha. Mr. McLean and Mike were busy preparing Blues King for the first race of the afternoon, the Sprint. Mr. Townsend had finally arrived, and he and Ashleigh went off to talk. Brad and Lavinia drifted around with their friends but stayed away from Pride's stall. Samantha was too busy, in any case, to pay much attention to them. She bathed and groomed Pride so that every inch of his copper coat gleamed. She and Tor took him for a short walk, but returned him to his stall when too many photographers started snapping his picture. Pride loved the attention, but Samantha knew he was getting too excited. He wouldn't be racing until late in the afternoon, and she didn't want him turning into a bundle of nerves.

Ashleigh returned from her talk with Mr. Townsend.

"How did it go?" Samantha asked quickly.

"Fine. He wasn't even considering scratching Pride, although he's not any happier about the post position than I am."

"Did he say anything about retiring Pride after the Classic?" Samantha asked.

"Not a word. The whole rumor was definitely another of Brad's mind games." Ashleigh checked her watch. "Mike must have brought Blues King up to the receiving barn already—the Sprint's in less than an hour. I'm a mess. I'm going to go change. I'll see you guys in the stands for the Sprint."

Len sat watch at Pride's stall when Samantha and Tor left to watch Blues King race. Jilly was riding and wearing Whitebrook's blue-and-white silks.

"I don't want to get my hopes up too high," Mike said as the field warmed up, "but I don't think he'll disgrace himself either. After the way he's been winning lately, he deserved a shot."

"He may surprise you," Ashleigh told him.

As they waited for the race to start, Samantha looked around at the overflowing grandstands and crowded infield. The day was overcast and chilly, but that hadn't stopped fans from coming for the Breeders' Cup. They were ready for a day of thrilling races, and if the Sprint was any indication, the day was going to be full of thrills.

Jilly got Blues King out sharply, and the two of them headed straight for the lead. Within strides of the gate they caught the lead horse, the second favorite in the field, and it was a two-horse race from then on. Blues King and By Your Leave ran neck and neck, leaving the rest of the field behind through the whole six-furlong race. The favorite in the race, the previous year's winner, never lifted a hoof. Samantha screamed out encouragement until she was hoarse. Mike couldn't seem to believe his eyes as Blues King continued vying for the lead. He jumped to his feet as the two horses pounded to the wire, head and head. Samantha held her breath. It was so close! It could go either way. Blues King at twenty-to-one odds looked like he was going to pull a huge upset. It was a head-bobbing finish, so close that a photo was called. They all waited tensely for the photo to be examined. In the end Blues King lost to By Your Leave by the barest nose. Blues King's performance was worth celebrating!

Samantha took her turn hugging Mike in congratulation. He seemed utterly stunned, but thrilled, by Blues King's effort. Then they all filed below to congratulate Jilly and the gelding as they came off the track.

Blues King's second-place finish in such a major race cheered everyone. But Samantha felt butterflies start fluttering in her stomach when they returned to the backside to await the time when Pride would race. The Classic was the last of the seven Breeders'

Cup races. The atmosphere on the backside was buzzing. While Mike took Ashleigh off for a walk, Tor stayed with Samantha as she put the finishing touches on Pride, then covered him with a green-and-gold Townsend Acres sheet and settled him in his stall. Tor suggested they take a walk themselves. "Len's here to keep an eye on him, and a walk might help your prerace jitters," he said with a teasing smile.

"And here I thought I was putting on such a good act of staying calm. A walk sounds like a good idea, though."

They set out through the barn area, checking out the rest of the field for the Classic. They paused by the stalls of Trompe and Mach Three, the European horses Ashleigh thought might pose a threat. "They both put in good workouts," Samantha said.

"But they're not that used to American tracks," Tor replied. "I'd be more concerned about Super Value. He's a known quantity."

"True," Samantha said. Super Value had raced against Pride before, and with his incredibly powerful closing kick he was always a threat. "And of course Lord Ainsley is a threat, especially after what Mike told us last night. I've been watching how the track's been playing. It seems to be favoring the rail. My guess is that LeBlanc will have Lord Ainsley right alongside it."

"We'll find out soon enough," Tor said. "We ought to be getting back."

"Right. Ashleigh will be taking Pride up to the receiving barn soon."

Ashleigh was talking to Len when Tor and Samantha returned. She was wearing a neat navy blue suit and looked very professional, but her forehead was furrowed in thought.

"Is it time to take him up?" Samantha asked.

"Just about," Ashleigh replied. Samantha went into the stall with a lead shank and led Pride out. He came eagerly. He always knew when he was racing and reacted with extra spark. He looked around with intelligent interest and flared his delicate nostrils. Samantha laid a proud hand on his glossy neck and gave his lead shank to Ashleigh.

Before Ashleigh led him off, she took Samantha's hand and squeezed it. "Here we go. See you in the saddling paddock."

Pride looked his magnificent best when Samantha led him around the walking ring. He was alert and composed and drew admiring calls from the crowd. But Lord Ainsley looked superb, too. Looking at him, Samantha had difficulty believing he might have trouble handling the track surface. Lavinia and Brad certainly seemed pleased and beamed out confident smiles as Maddock gave instructions to Lord Ainsley's jockey.

Samantha studied each of the horses in the field as she and Pride circled the ring. Super Value, Trompe, and Mach Three all looked in top form—calm and ready to put their minds to business. There was only one true speed horse in the race, Costar, but Samantha noticed he was already breaking out in a sweat, and unless something extraordinary happened, she doubted he could hold out for the full mile and a quarter. More likely he would tire and start fading in the stretch. Of course, none of the horses in the field were slouches. They were all winners of graded stakes or they wouldn't have made it into the field of the Classic.

When Samantha, Tor, and Ashleigh finally climbed to their reserved seating to watch the race, the field for the Classic was coming onto the track. Mike and the others were already in their seats. As Samantha sat down, Tor reached over and took her icy fingers in his own and held them reassuringly.

"Relax," Tor whispered to her. "I know how you're feeling, but Pride looks great. He and Jilly will give it their best."

Samantha gave him a watery smile and returned the squeeze of his fingers. She always hated these moments of tense anticipation waiting for the start of a race. She felt like her stomach was in her throat.

The horses were loading. Jilly and Pride, who would load last, circled as they waited for their turn to go into the auxiliary gate. Samantha wondered what thoughts were going through Jilly's mind. Was she already concentrating on the break from the gate, which would have to be incredibly fast? Was she feeling any of the nervous trepidation Samantha was feeling?

Samantha was barely breathing as Pride and Jilly finally loaded in the fourteen slot. Pride went in calmly. The attendants closed the doors behind them. Jilly had only seconds to settle herself before the track announcer cried, "And they're off for the running of the Breeders' Cup Classic! Costar and Lord Ainsley break sharply from the inside. Trompe and Mach Three are both after the early lead, and Wonder's Pride is out quickly and gaining ground from the far-outside post position. Mari's Pleasure is off a beat slow."

Samantha expelled a breath of relief. Pride had broken sharply. That was one big obstacle out of the way, but could he make it across the track in front of a dozen other horses to get up with the leaders?

"And as they head past the stands for the first time," the announcer continued, "it's Costar with a short lead, Trompe on his outside, and Mach Three running with him—three of them across the track. Lord Ainsley is tucked in behind, saving ground on the rail. Jilly Gordon angles Wonder's Pride across the track, but with so much ground to make up, the best they can do is to settle into fifth on the outside. Super Value, as usual, is content to trail the field, ten lengths off the leaders."

Samantha had unconsciously slid to the end of her seat, her eyes glued to the track. Pride was set to run, but the three lead horses formed a wall in front of him across the track. He had no place to go.

"As they go into the clubhouse turn Costar, Trompe, and Mach Three are fighting it out for the lead!" the announcer cried. "They're running neck and neck, none of them giving an inch, and they're setting *bristling* fractions—twenty-two seconds for the first quarter! Lord Ainsley and Wonder's Pride are just behind them, the five leaders bunched with only a length separating them. After a slow start Mari's Pleasure is two lengths back in sixth, then Redeemable . . ."

Samantha tuned out the announcer and concentrated on the five lead horses. Their positions remained unchanged as they moved around the clubhouse turn. "Sit cool, Jilly," Samantha murmured under her breath. She knew how much Pride hated being stuck behind a wall of horses. Jilly had two options—to sit tight and wait for the front-running horses to tire and for a gap to open, or to move Pride out and around them, four wide, and take the chance of getting involved in a speed duel. A speed duel this early in the race could be suicidal and leave Pride's tank on empty coming down the stretch. Samantha could guess the strategy of the jockeys on the front-running horses was to keep Pride off the lead as long as possible, hoping that when he was finally able to make a move, it would be too late.

The leaders pounded down the backstretch. The pace was taking its toll on Costar. He started to fade and drifted out just enough to leave a narrow gap on the rail. LeBlanc wasted no time. He urged Lord Ainsley through, and they shot forward to take a short lead over Trompe and Mach

Three. Pride was still stuck behind.

Samantha grimaced and heard Ashleigh's quiet groan. "LeBlanc's sure running this one right. He's using the track bias to Lord Ainsley's advantage. They haven't had to move off the rail once."

"He took a chance of getting boxed in, though," Samantha said.

"Yeah, but it paid off, didn't it?"

The announcer's voice was growing increasingly excited. "As they approach the far turn Lord Ainsley continues to hold a short lead. Trompe and Mach Three neck and neck for second. Wonder's Pride is blocked behind them and will have to go four wide to get around. Costar back in fifth, then Mari's Pleasure, Redeemable . . . and Super Value has found his best stride and is gaining on the outside!"

"Take him around!" Ashleigh muttered. "Before Super Value gets up and blocks you in."

Samantha saw that Jilly was preparing to do just that. She had started angling Pride out around Mach Three, four wide, when Mach Three suddenly lunged out, right into her and Pride's intended path. Samantha and Ashleigh both gasped. Samantha could imagine the thoughts going through Jilly's mind. The jockey was going to have to act fast to avoid Pride running right up on Mach Three's heels.

Jilly was forced to check hard, shortening Pride's stride and losing their momentum. She quickly tightened her left rein, urging Pride inside of Mach Three.

Seconds later Pride was back in stride again, but Lord Ainsley and Trompe had increased their lead on the field to two lengths. Super Value continued his drive on the outside, passing tiring horses, and was only a couple of lengths behind Pride. But Pride was striding out again after the leaders.

The announcer was nearly screaming in his excitement as the horses went around the far turn. "Lord Ainsley is still in the lead. Trompe is a half-length back in second. After being checked, Wonder's Pride is in pursuit another two lengths back, and Super Value is making a big move on the outside, now up in fourth. And *down* the stretch they come!"

Samantha cringed to see that Lord Ainsley was actually increasing his lead as he powered toward the wire. But Pride was still coming on, accelerating into a higher gear after changing leads. He and Jilly edged past Trompe into second.

"A sixteenth of a mile to go!" the announcer screeched. "Can Wonder's Pride catch Lord Ainsley?"

With her heart in her throat, Samantha watched Pride gradually eat into Lord Ainsley's lead. "Come on, Pride!" she shouted. "Get him!" Would Pride have time? The wire was coming much too quickly. She saw LeBlanc glance under his arm. He went to his whip on Lord Ainsley, but Pride was still coming like a freight train. Samantha knew the heart and will that were driving Pride. She knew by now that he didn't need Jilly's encouragement. He was striving to win on his own. She loved him all the more for it—even if he couldn't get up to beat Lord Ainsley.

Samantha and Tor were on their feet, as were the others, screaming their encouragement as Pride moved up even with Lord Ainsley. Super Value was still coming on and was just off Pride's flank. The race could go to any of them. The roar from the crowd was deafening.

Strides from the wire, Pride reached down for an extra reserve. With a powerful lunge he thundered past Lord Ainsley to take the lead. Pride and Jilly swept past the finish a length in front!

"He did it!" Samantha screamed, gripping Tor in a bear hug.

"He won the Classic! What a race! What an incredible race!"

Tor laughed as he returned her hug. Samantha turned to Ashleigh. Ashleigh's eyes were bright with unshed tears of happiness and relief.

"Wasn't he wonderful, Sammy?" Ashleigh cried. "Wasn't he amazing?"

"There's no question about that," Mike said.

They were mobbed by press and fans as they made their way down to the track. In the winner's circle they met a beaming Clay Townsend, who took both of Ashleigh's hands and congratulated her. There was no sign of Lavinia or Brad, even though the television commentators were giving Lord Ainsley his share of plaudits for having run a superb race. It was totally unlike them not to show up for the cameras to share in the honors for Townsend Acres.

"So," a smiling commentator said to Ashleigh and Mr. Townsend, "it looks like he's just clinched Horse of the Year honors."

"And deserves them," Mr. Townsend said.

"Now that I have both his owners here," the commentator continued, "can you confirm the rumor that this was Wonder's Pride's last race—that he's headed for retirement?"

"I think Ashleigh will agree that we'd like to enjoy *this* moment," Mr. Townsend said firmly. "There will be plenty of time later to talk of any possible retirement."

Listening, Samantha breathed a sigh of relief, but she realized Mr. Townsend hadn't given a firm no either. She put it out of her mind as she gave Pride a congratulatory kiss and held him while the photographs were taken. The crowds were going wild with raves for Pride.

Ashleigh, Mr. Townsend, and Jilly would remain for the presentation ceremony. Moments later Samantha led Pride off past his cheering fans toward the backside. Tor, Yvonne and Gregg, and Mr. McLean and Beth walked with her. Pride had his neck arched and he pranced for his admirers. It was his crowning moment, and Samantha's heart swelled with joy.

There was still no sign of Lavinia or Brad when they reached their barn. Hank was already sponging down Lord Ainsley at the end of the shedrow. Ken Maddock was with him. As Samantha led Pride toward his stall and prepared to unsheet him, several grooms from other stables came over to congratulate Pride.

"Great race!" one of them said. "But Lavinia Townsend sure took her horse's losing pretty hard. She came running through here after the race in tears. Her husband was trying to calm her down."

Samantha turned and looked at Yvonne and Tor. Lavinia in tears? "I don't believe it," Samantha said.

10

ASHLEIGH AND MIKE RETURNED TO THE BACKSIDE AFTER
Samantha had finished bathing and cooling out
Pride and had him back in his stall. It hadn't been an
easy task, with all the people who came by to congratulate them and see how Pride had come out of
the race. Samantha and Len had both checked him
over carefully, and the big chestnut seemed fine after
all his efforts.

Ashleigh went in to check Pride over herself and came
out of the stall smiling. "It hasn't really sunk in yet," she
said. "He just won the Classic! He's guaranteed to be
named Horse of the Year! Wow! I can't stop smiling."

"And why should you?" Mike said with a grin.
"You deserve to smile after what you've been
through the last six months."

"Speaking of the last six months," Ashleigh said,
"I heard a rumor that Lavinia was in tears after the
race."

105

"That's what the grooms told us," Samantha confirmed.

"She's taking it that hard?" Mike asked. "Lord Ainsley ran a darn good race, in spite of the fact that Pride beat him."

"I don't think Lavinia sees it that way," Samantha said. "All she cared about was winning."

"Or could her tears be a big act?" Yvonne asked.

"But why? What's she going to gain?"

"Sympathy from her father-in-law," Yvonne said.

"Come on, guys," Tor interrupted, "aren't we being a little too mean and cynical? Why shouldn't she be upset enough to break down? This was an important race for them."

"I suppose," Yvonne agreed. "But it isn't like her."

Mr. Townsend approached, looking elated. "That's the most press coverage we've received since Pride won the Derby," he said. "They wouldn't leave me alone."

"I know," Ashleigh said. "Mike and I practically had to sneak away."

"How's Pride come out of the race?" Mr. Townsend asked.

"Well, very well. He doesn't seem too exhausted, and he's already digging into his dinner."

Mr. Townsend nodded. "Good. He ran an absolutely fantastic race. He's a real credit to us."

"I heard Lavinia was pretty upset after the race," Ashleigh said.

"Unfortunately she took Lord Ainsley's defeat pretty hard," Mr. Townsend answered. "Understandable. She and Brad put a lot of work into the colt and had their hopes up pretty high. That's the difficulty of having two good horses from the same stable competing against each other."

"Lord Ainsley ran a very good race," Ashleigh said. "Especially since he didn't really care for the track surface."

"Oh, I know," Mr. Townsend agreed. "Brad and Lavinia have nothing to be embarrassed about. He's a darned good horse, and there's always next year. Both he and Pride can take a well-deserved rest. I'll be heading out now." He took Ashleigh's hand. "You did a wonderful job bringing him up to the race. Congratulations and thanks. To you, too, Sammy." With a parting smile, he left to go talk to Ken Maddock.

"What a nice man," Yvonne said. "How did he turn out a son like Brad?"

Relieved to have the prerace pressure off and buoyed by Pride's success, they all returned to Whitebrook. Pride got his well-deserved rest. Samantha put him out in the pasture every day while the November weather stayed decent. He had nothing to do but graze and romp over the still-green grass. There had been no killing frosts yet. Samantha watched him from the paddock fence, feeling a little awed and very lucky that she had a part in the career of this fantastic horse. Pride would have nearly two months of rest before going back in training again in January, but Ashleigh was already talking excitedly about the following year's schedule, possibly entering Pride in the Grade 1 Santa Anita Handicap in California in March.

In the weeks following their return, Ashleigh was swamped with mail from Pride's fans, and the papers were comparing him to Secretariat, although Samantha realized he hadn't quite reached that status yet. Maureen ran Samantha's column on the Breeders' Cup as a feature article in the school paper, and tons of kids stopped Samantha to tell her they'd seen the race and to congratulate her. And Pride wasn't the only one getting attention. After Blues King's impressive performance, Mike was receiving calls from owners interested in training their horses at Whitebrook. All in all, things couldn't have been better.

Ashleigh and Mike went to Louisville for her sister Caroline's wedding to Justin McGowan. Since the mid-November weather continued to be mild, Samantha invited Tor, Yvonne, and Gregg over to Whitebrook for a ride. Sierra had recovered enough from his pulled muscle that Tor thought an easy trail ride would do him good, and Samantha rode Pride. Everyone had a ball. They talked about Yvonne and Tor's plans for Cisco and Top Hat; Ashleigh and Samantha's plans for Pride; the college applications Samantha, Yvonne, and Gregg were sending out. Yvonne was thrilled because with hard work on her part, she had brought up her grades to a B average for the first quarter. She was trying to keep them there.

"I'm kind of nervous about midterms, though," Yvonne told them. "I freak at big tests—my mind goes blank."

"You don't have to worry about that until after Christmas and New Year's," Samantha said. "Speaking of Christmas, Tor and I have been thinking of putting on a small Christmas show and party at the stable for the disabled riders. They're all doing so well, and showing off to their families and friends should boost their confidence even more."

"I think it's a great idea!" Yvonne said. "Some of them are already good enough to ride without a lead rein—Robert, and Aaron and Charmaine—and Mandy, of course. What do you say, Gregg? Would you have time to help?"

"Sure," Gregg said. "Did you pick a date?"

"Well, it'll definitely be a Saturday so it's easier for the parents to come," Tor said. "How about two weeks before Christmas?"

"Sounds good."

"Beth is coming over to have dinner with us tonight," Samantha said. "I'll talk to her about it. We'll have another month to practice with the kids. Maybe we should have the lessons once a week until the show."

"If Beth and Janet can arrange to get everyone to the stable, that sounds fine to me," Tor agreed.

That night when Samantha talked to Beth about their idea for a show, Beth was filled with enthusiasm. "It's a wonderful idea. They'll love it. I'm sure Janet will like the idea, too. Just tell me what I can do to help."

"Well, we probably could use some help with the refreshments," Samantha suggested, knowing how Beth loved to cook.

"I'll take care of it," Beth said eagerly.

A few days later Clay Townsend stopped by Whitebrook to see Wonder, Pride, and Mr. Wonderful. Samantha was inside Pride's stall, grooming him, as Ashleigh and Mr. Townsend paused outside.

"He's enjoying his time off," Ashleigh said cheerfully, "and you can see how fit he's looking. I thought I'd put him back in serious training in early January."

Mr. Townsend suddenly looked troubled. "I wanted to talk to you about that, Ashleigh," he said. "Since the Breeders' Cup, I've been giving more thought to Pride's future. Now that he's won the Classic and is pretty much guaranteed Horse of the Year honors, maybe it is time to consider retiring him to stud—while he's at his absolute peak."

At his words, Samantha froze with her brush in midair. Ashleigh's face had fallen. "But when we talked after the Classic, you seemed to be thinking ahead to his five-year-old season!" Ashleigh exclaimed. "And Pride is certainly fit and capable of running another year."

"Yes, I *was* thinking ahead to next year," Mr. Townsend admitted. "But I've had some second thoughts. My son and daughter-in-law have reminded me that now would probably be the best time to retire him. He's at the top of the game. With his record and breeding, especially if he's named Horse of the Year, we can demand and get top stud fees. If

110

he's retired now, he would be available for this year's breeding season. I've already had inquiries from people wanting to reserve bookings for their mares."

"But what about the purses he'd win if he raced another year?" Ashleigh argued. "They'd be equal to any stud fees. I'd like to enter him in the Santa Anita Handicap. That's a million-dollar purse right there."

"But as fit as he seems, there's no guarantee he'll *win* his races next year," Mr. Townsend said, "and there's always the possibility of injury. We're looking at stud fees in the range of thirty thousand dollars per live foal. Since he could be bred to up to fifty mares, that's nothing to sneeze at."

"He'll still be in huge demand at stud if he races another year," Ashleigh said.

"But possibly not for as high a fee if he puts in a poor season. The stud fees he'd bring now are guaranteed. There's no guarantee that he'll win big purses. It's a fickle market—who knows what breeders will be willing to pay in another year? And by racing him, there's always the risk of serious, even fatal injury. It just seems to make more sense to retire him now—not only for economical reasons, but for practical ones—for his own well-being."

"I need to think about it," Ashleigh said tightly. Samantha could see how furious Ashleigh was, especially knowing who was pushing the idea of Pride's early retirement. Would Mr. Townsend have even considered it if Lavinia and Brad hadn't made it an issue?

"There's still a month and a half until breeding

season begins," Mr. Townsend said, "although I would like to make a decision before that. Think about it and let me know. I'll be in town for the next few weeks. I know it's a difficult decision, but I hope we can reach an agreement."

Samantha hurried to the stall door when Mr. Townsend had left. "You're not going to agree to retire him, are you?" she asked breathlessly.

"Not without a fight," Ashleigh replied. "I know Pride will be retired eventually, but I also know Mr. Townsend was all set to race him another year—until Brad and Lavinia got to him. I'll bet there hasn't been any talk of retiring Lord Ainsley, and he and Pride are both four. Lavinia and Brad just want Pride out of the way so that Lord Ainsley will shine."

Later that afternoon Hank came by Whitebrook to visit Len. He scowled when they told him about Mr. Townsend's decision.

"I was hoping it wouldn't come to that," Hank said. "I heard Brad and Lavinia talking to him about next year's breeding season. She's been moping around since the Breeders' Cup, sticking her nose in everyone's business. She and Brad were really after Townsend to think of retiring Pride, reminding him how Townsend Acres would benefit financially from a new stallion of Pride's caliber in the barn. They'd already worked up a bunch of figures." He made a scoffing noise. "Lavinia even suggested that Pride could stand at the new Townsend Acres operation in England, but Townsend Senior wouldn't even consider it."

112

"That witch!" Ashleigh exclaimed. "She knows how much that would upset me. I should have figured Mr. Townsend would want Pride to stand at Townsend Acres."

"Pride would be moved to Townsend Acres?" Samantha cried, feeling her heart sink. She couldn't bear the thought of Pride being taken from Whitebrook. It would be absolutely terrible!

"Not if I can help it," Ashleigh said tightly. "Don't worry, Sammy, I haven't agreed to anything yet. I'm hoping Mr. Townsend will change his mind. I think he's wrong, but I need to get my arguments together, too, before I talk to him again." Ashleigh paused, scowling angrily, then looked over to Hank. "How's Princess doing?"

"Good. She's gone out on the track a couple of times with the other yearlings—with one of the regular exercise riders in the saddle. I haven't let Lavinia near her," Hank added quickly when he saw Ashleigh's worried expression. "Princess has taken to the routine and seems to be putting her mind to business. We'll be finishing up the yearling training this week, and give them a break until January. We're running late as it is, but with over a dozen yearlings to train, it takes time."

"Is Lavinia still trying to turn herself into an exercise rider?" Samantha asked.

"Oh, yeah. Brad even let her up on one of his three-year-olds. Maddock didn't look too happy about it, but she managed to get the colt through the workout without any disasters. Can't say I think much of her riding, though. She's got terrible hands and bullies the horses around."

"Just as long as she stays away from Princess," Ashleigh said.

"Brad isn't going to put her up on a green yearling. Even he knows better than that."

Beth told Samantha that Janet was thrilled with the idea of a Christmas show and party, and that Wednesday when Samantha and Tor told the children, their eyes sparkled.

"But I'm going to be nervous!" Jane said.

"You won't have to do anything too hard," Tor reassured her. "Just the things we've been doing in our lessons, and you'll have plenty of time to practice, starting right now," he added with a grin. "Everybody ready? We're going to have all of you walk your ponies around the ring without leading reins today. You lead out, Timmy. We'll be right here if anyone needs help."

Samantha watched with a smile as the children urged their ponies around the ring. Several of the ponies balked, but Tor called out encouragement. After six sessions the children were all gaining confidence and looked forward excitedly to their afternoon at the stable. Samantha noticed that Aaron, who was so sad eyed during their first session, now wore a bright smile as he urged his pony on. Samantha was especially impressed with Mandy Jarvis. The little girl loved riding and was always eager to try something new. She had really taken a shine to Samantha and looked at her with awestruck eyes. "I saw you on television!" Mandy had told Samantha when Samantha had helped her onto her pony. "Your horse is so beautiful!"

"He's not actually my horse," Samantha said with a smile. "I'm just his groom. But I love him. He's very special to me."

"And you ride him. Someday I'm going to ride like you. That's my dream."

Samantha was flattered by Mandy's admiration. She only prayed that Mandy's dream would come true, because, despite the little girl's spirit and enthusiasm, there was no guarantee Mandy would recover full use of her legs.

After the lesson was over and the children had been escorted back to the van, Samantha talked to Tor about Mr. Townsend's visit the previous day. "I don't know what Ashleigh can do to convince him to change his mind," she said.

"I know how disappointed you'd be if Pride is retired," Tor said as they led the ponies from the ring. "But Townsend does have a point. There's always the danger of injury if Pride keeps racing."

Samantha gave him a startled look.

"I'm not saying I'd like to see Pride retired," Tor said quickly. "I'd like to see him race another year, too. The fans love him. He's a real boost to the racing industry. There will be a lot of disappointed people if he's retired."

"And a couple of very happy ones," Samantha said with a frown. "It's not just the talk of retirement that upsets me. I would absolutely die if they took Pride to Townsend Acres!"

"I can't see Ashleigh willingly agreeing to that. She may be able to change Mr. Townsend's mind. Whitebrook is smaller than Townsend Acres, but you do have excellent breeding facilities, and Townsend Acres would still get half the stud fees. How long does Ashleigh have to decide?"

"Only a couple of weeks."

The next morning the temperature fell to near freezing. After Samantha had fed and groomed Pride and put him out in the paddock with a warm blanket covering him, she stopped by Mike's office to see if Ashleigh was there. She wanted to talk to Ashleigh before she left for school.

Both Mike and Ashleigh were inside. When Ashleigh looked up, her face was pale and drawn, and Mike looked furious.

"Is something wrong?" Samantha asked in alarm.

"I just got some really bad news," Ashleigh replied tightly.

"About Pride's retirement?"

Ashleigh shook her head. "Hank just called. Princess has been injured."

Samantha gasped. "Oh, no! What happened?"

Anger flashed in Ashleigh's eyes. "Lavinia took her out on the track for her last work. Hank had no idea what Lavinia was up to. He didn't find out until afterward. Maddock had another rider assigned to Princess, but Lavinia told Maddock she was acting on

Brad's authority, and she would ride. Maddock didn't like it, but he couldn't stop her. Neither Brad nor Mr. Townsend was at the farm."

Samantha groaned, imagining what was coming next.

"Lavinia couldn't handle Princess," Ashleigh continued. "She's never ridden a green horse, but, being Lavinia, she was too cocky to listen to Maddock. Princess bolted with her halfway through the workout, took a misstep, and fell. Lavinia wasn't hurt except for a couple of bruises, but Princess fractured a bone in her foreleg. It's not life threatening. The vet says the fracture will heal, but Princess may *never* be able to race, and if she does, her training will be put back months!"

Samantha leaned against the wall of the office. She felt like she'd had the wind knocked out of her. "Are you going over there?" she asked.

"Yes. I'm heading out now," Ashleigh said. "Hank said the vet had put a temporary cast on her leg, and they were going to van her over to his clinic. I've never heard Hank so upset."

Mike clenched his jaw. "With good reason!"

Samantha hated having to leave for school. When she met Yvonne and Maureen before homeroom, she told them what had happened to Princess. They were both horrified. It was going to be a busy day at school. Samantha had a trig test second period, an English assignment to research in the library, and a newspaper staff meeting right after school. She had a tough time concentrating and spent most of the day worrying about Princess and anxiously wondering what was going on at Townsend Acres.

As soon as she got home that afternoon she rushed to Mike's office, hoping to find Ashleigh there. She was, and she and Mike didn't look much happier than they had that morning.

"How's Princess?" Samantha asked.

"They've brought her over to the clinic," Ashleigh said. "She was uncomfortable when I saw her, but Hank went over to the clinic with her."

"What about Lavinia?" Samantha asked. "Did you see her?"

"You bet I did! She'd already gone up to the main house to nurse her bruises, but I was so angry, I went up after her. Brad and Mr. Townsend weren't back yet. I really laid into her. I don't remember half of what I said, but I think she was terrified I was going to hit her." Ashleigh gave a wry smile. "She knew she'd been in the wrong, but of course, she wouldn't admit it. She said the accident was *Princess's* fault—that the filly was unmanageable. I left before I really did hit her." Ashleigh paused. "When I got back to the stable area, Brad was there and had heard the news. He tried to defend Lavinia, but you could tell he was only trying to cover for her. He knew she'd been totally in the wrong. And because Lavinia insisted on riding, one of the most promising yearlings in the stable might never race."

"What about Mr. Townsend?"

"He still wasn't back at Townsend Acres," Ashleigh said, "but I can pretty much imagine

118

what he'll have to say when he finds out—unless Lavinia succeeds in disguising the facts."

"I don't see that happening," Mike put in. "Ken Maddock saw the whole thing. He didn't want Lavinia to ride."

The office phone rang, and Mike picked it up. "She's right here, Mr. Townsend," he said a second later, and handed Ashleigh the phone.

Ashleigh listened for several moments. "I realize you're as upset as I am, Mr. Townsend, and I appreciate your calling. . . . I certainly hope nothing like this happens again, but it's a little late for Princess. . . . Yes, I know Hank will give her the best of care. I think the world of Hank. I'm not faulting him. What infuriates me is that a promising filly that I co-own may have been ruined because of the irresponsible actions of your daughter-in-law, and if this is the kind of thing that's going to happen, I don't want Princess at Townsend Acres. . . . I don't think I'll feel any less upset in the morning. . . . All right. Good night, Mr. Townsend."

Samantha and Mike waited as Ashleigh hung up the phone. "So?" Mike finally asked.

"He only got home a half-hour ago. He's furious. He said he's talked to both Lavinia and Brad—that something like this won't happen again. He understands how I feel about leaving Princess at Townsend Acres, but he wants me to think about it after I calm down. Ha! Like I'm suddenly going to start putting my trust in those two?"

"With Princess injured, and if Pride is retired, you

won't have any of your own horses running next year," Samantha said.

"Right," Ashleigh answered with disgust. "And that's just what Lavinia wants. I'm sick to death of the two of them coming up smelling like roses all the time!"

11

YVONNE AND MAUREEN WERE WAITING FOR SAMANTHA when she arrived at school the next morning. She gave them an update on Princess as they walked to their lockers. "I don't believe Lavinia!" Yvonne cried angrily. "And she's not even sorry?"

"According to her, it was Princess's fault," Samantha said.

Yvonne rolled her eyes.

"It's just amazing how much trouble they cause!" Maureen exclaimed, distractedly pushing her glasses up on her nose. "When will it stop? Ashleigh should stick to her guns, though, and refuse to retire Pride."

"After this, I think she will," Samantha said.

"I know how bummed out you're feeling," Yvonne said, "but maybe you should go out and have some fun. I'm trying to get a bunch of us together to go bowling tomorrow night. Why don't you and Tor come?"

"Bowling?" Samantha said. "I haven't gone bowling in—I don't know how long, and I wasn't very good then!"

"It'll be fun," Yvonne told her. "So what if we all make jerks out of ourselves."

"Okay, it does sound like fun," Samantha agreed. "I'll call Tor when I get home this afternoon."

Yvonne had managed to get five couples to the bowling alley Saturday night. They split up into two teams and had a hilarious time. There were plenty of gutter balls thrown, but every so often someone bowled incredibly well. Samantha sat down in shock when she rolled two strikes in a row.

"Just an accident," she said with a grin when her teammates congratulated her. "I haven't got a clue what I was doing right."

"Just keep it up," Tor told her happily. "We're in the lead."

Unfortunately they didn't stay in the lead, but they didn't lose by much. Afterward they all went out for pizza. When Tor brought Samantha home an hour later, Samantha knew the night out had done her good. She was still troubled by Princess's injury and Pride's possible retirement. The horses, especially Pride, were such a big part of her life, it was impossible not to let the disappointments get to her. But it had been a great night. She wasn't feeling quite so down. Tor understood how she was feeling and had done his best all night to cheer her up.

"You're smiling again," he said to her as they strolled arm in arm through the barns before he headed home. With Sierra out of training, Tor hadn't been spending as much time at Whitebrook. He spent most of his free time now working with Top Hat so they would be ready for the National Horse Show in February. "Not that you don't have plenty of reason to feel bummed," he added. "I would be, too. We'll just have to think positively."

Samantha looked up at him and smiled. "Princess's leg will heal quickly, and Mr. Townsend will change his mind about retiring Pride."

"That's the way," Tor said with a twinkle in his eyes.

Only the night-lights were burning in the stables. They stopped to see Pride and Sierra, who were both dozing, then walked over to the mares and weanlings' barn, pausing to look in on Mr. Wonderful and Precocious. "They're turning into beauties, aren't they?" Samantha said proudly.

"They sure are."

"And after what happened to Princess, I think Mr. Townsend will agree to let Mr. Wonderful be trained here."

"That's one piece of good news," Tor said.

Samantha nodded. "Let's go see Wonder, then I'd better go in, or I won't want to get up in the morning."

They all tried to make Thanksgiving a festive affair, but it wasn't easy. Beth, who loved to cook, made a spectacular dinner in the Reeses' kitchen, shooing Ashleigh and Samantha away when they offered to help. Tor and his father and Ashleigh's parents joined the rest of the Whitebrook staff as they sat down at the long table in the dining room. Ashleigh's sister, Caroline, and her new husband were having Thanksgiving with his family, and her brother, Rory, was at his girlfriend's.

"I'm sorry it's been such a tough month for you, Ashleigh," Mr. Griffen said to his daughter. "Any news on Princess?"

"Hank called yesterday. She's back at Townsend Acres. The vet put a pin in her foreleg to stabilize the fracture, and she's in a half-cast. She's able to walk around. Of course, until the fracture heals, no one knows if she'll be able to race."

"Have you made any decision about retiring Pride?"

"I don't want to retire him," Ashleigh said, "but I don't know how easy it will be to get Mr. Townsend to see my point of view. My only real hope is that Mr. Townsend hadn't originally wanted to retire Pride— until Lavinia and Brad started pestering him. Pride couldn't be in better shape. He wasn't overraced last year. He's at the top of his game—and he's the only one of Wonder's offspring that will be able to race this year. I know Mr. Townsend is thinking of the stud fees he'll bring, but I truly believe that Pride will keep winning big races. He loves it! He's in his glory when he's out on the track."

"He might enjoy the company of a few mares, too," Mr. Reese said teasingly.

"I'm sure he would, but he'll have plenty of time for that after he races another year." Then Ashleigh sobered. "They want him to stand stud at Townsend

Acres, which I am dead against! I don't want him anywhere near Lavinia and Brad. Lavinia's already messed up Princess."

"What if you can't convince Mr. Townsend?" Mr. Griffen asked.

"Then I guess we'll do battle," Ashleigh said. "He can't retire Pride without my cooperation."

"And you'll have difficulty racing Pride without *his* cooperation," her father reminded her.

"True, but I'm going to try my darnedest to get him to change his mind."

"Just as long as you don't let your dislike for them affect your judgment," Mrs. Griffen gently warned. "I'm just as angry at their tricks as you are. But Pride's well-being is the important thing."

"I *am* thinking of Pride," Ashleigh said. But Samantha saw the expression on Ashleigh's face and knew Mrs. Griffen's warning had upset her.

Later, as they were clearing the table, Ashleigh took Samantha aside. "Do *you* think I'm making the right decision, Sammy? Am I just being stubborn?"

"I don't think you're being stubborn," Samantha said. "I'd do the same thing you are. It would be different if Pride seemed worn-out and tired. But he's not. He loves racing, and it's not just you and me who want to see him keep going. He's special to so many people. He gives people something to believe in—something to admire. He makes them happy. Kids at school who never were the least bit interested in racing come up to me and tell me they think Pride's great—that they follow all his races.

They want to know everything about him and what it's like to be his groom. It's amazing."

Ashleigh was silent for a moment, lost in thought. "I know what you mean, Sammy," she said. "He *is* special. People love him. Mike tells me Pride is the best advertising the racing industry has had in years. He's an honest horse, who shows real courage on the track." Ashleigh paused, then looked at Samantha. "So you think I should stick to my guns."

"Yes, I do."

Samantha was jolted awake early the next morning by a steady pounding on the cottage door. It was still dark out. She sat up in bed and looked at the illuminated dial on her alarm clock. Only a quarter to four. She turned on her bedroom light and swung her legs over the side of her bed as the pounding continued. Seconds later her father stepped into the upstairs hall, still pulling on his bathrobe. Samantha thrust her arms into her own robe, and they both hurried downstairs. Samantha was still dazed from sleep and wondered what could be wrong—*Not a fire!* she prayed.

Her father pulled open the front door. Len was on the stoop.

Beyond him, Samantha saw the lights blazing in the mares' barn.

"It's Wonder," Len said. "I think she's going into early labor. I couldn't sleep and went out early to check the horses. Good thing I did. I already told Ashleigh."

Samantha pushed past Len and raced to the mares' barn. She was still in her robe but didn't even notice the chill night air. Ashleigh was already in Wonder's stall.

Samantha saw that Wonder was definitely in distress. She stood with her head lowered, breathing heavily. Samantha unlatched the door and joined Ashleigh inside. Wonder gave a soft nicker of greeting, then grunted again. Samantha rubbed her hand over the mare's neck. It was damp with sweat. "Do you really think it's early labor?" she asked Ashleigh.

"I'm almost positive. So was Len. Mike's father's on his way out. Mike went to call the vet."

"But she's four months early."

"I know. And I don't know if a foal born that premature can survive. Easy, girl," Ashleigh whispered to Wonder. "Help's coming. It's going to be all right."

Mr. Reese, who supervised the breeding operations on the farm, rushed into the barn. It was obvious he'd pulled on whatever clothes were closest to hand.

"She's been grunting in pain, and she's covered with sweat," Ashleigh explained quickly.

Mr. Reese went to Wonder's side. Len and Mr. McLean waited outside the stall. "She was just fine when I checked her for the last time tonight," Len said anxiously, as if he were somehow to blame.

"She's not doing too good now," Mr. Reese replied as he examined Wonder. "She may be miscarrying."

Mike returned to the stall. "Dr. Mendez is on his way," he said.

"Give me a hand, will you, Len?" Mr. Reese said as Wonder curled her legs under her and lay down on the bedding. Samantha left the stall to be out of the men's way. Ashleigh knelt in the straw beside Wonder and cradled the mare's head. Samantha heard Mr. Reese murmur to Len, "No question she's miscarrying. It'll be a miracle if she produces a foal this early on that can survive."

Ashleigh looked stricken, as if she was sharing Wonder's pain. Samantha felt helpless. All she could do was watch numbly.

The minutes dragged past, and Samantha's fears grew. When the vet finally hurried into the barn, he confirmed what Mr. Reese and Len thought. By now there was no question that Wonder was in the throes of premature labor. Samantha watched with growing dread as Wonder strained and whinnied anxiously, lifting her head from the straw with each contraction of her abdomen. Ashleigh continued to soothe her, her eyes brimming with tears.

Finally a small bundle, still covered by the birth sack, slipped from Wonder's body. The vet quickly knelt to examine it and pulled away the birth sack. Samantha felt a spurt of hope. Was there a possibility the foal was alive? She saw the same hope on Ashleigh's face.

"Stillborn," Dr. Mendez said a moment later. "A colt."

Tears welled in Samantha's eyes and she swallowed hard. Ashleigh let out a choked sob. Samantha couldn't bear to look at the pathetic little bundle on the straw.

"The foal would never have made it anyway," the

vet said to Ashleigh. His tone was kindly and sympathetic. "It's underdeveloped, and there are deformities to the legs. It's difficult to accept, I know, but it's better that she miscarried."

"And Wonder? Is she going to be all right?"

"We'll do everything to see that she is. She may have been carrying the dead foal for several days. If there's no infection . . . but before I leave, I'll take a blood sample to test."

Len had bundled up the tiny foal and rose to carry it from the stall. Wonder whinnied, knowing something was wrong. "Easy, girl, easy," Ashleigh soothed brokenly.

Samantha felt dazed and sick. They all stayed by Wonder's stall as the vet continued to minister to Wonder and the afterbirth was cleanly delivered. Dr. Mendez took a blood sample and gave Wonder a shot of antibiotics. "Just in case," he said. "I'd say she's going to be all right. I'll wait until she's back on her feet. Someone should keep an eye on her during the rest of the night."

"I'll stay with her," Ashleigh said.

To everyone's relief, Wonder gradually seemed to be recovering as she would after a normal birth. She finally gathered her legs beneath her and rose to her feet, but she seemed confused and disoriented, as if her instincts told her she'd just delivered a foal needing her care—but there was no foal. She looked anxiously around the stall and sniffed the air. Only Ashleigh's soothing words seemed to settle her down. Len brought a clean warm blanket, which

Ashleigh fastened over Wonder's back.

"That's all I can do for now," the vet said. "Call me if there's any change for the worse. I'll stop by tomorrow to check on her." He gathered up his instruments. Mr. Reese walked him out to his car.

"Do you want me to stay with you?" Samantha asked Ashleigh.

Ashleigh wearily shook her head. "No. Mike's going to stay. Try and get some sleep. We're all going to be exhausted tomorrow as it is."

"If you're sure," Samantha said. She realized she would be of more help to Ashleigh after a few more hours sleep—if she *could* sleep.

Samantha dragged herself out of bed three hours later. Her father was in the kitchen finishing his coffee when she came downstairs. "Have you been out to see Wonder yet?" she asked.

"I was just on my way. How are you doing, Sammy?"

At her father's concern Samantha again felt the hot sting of tears in her eyes. "I'm feeling pretty bad. Everyone had such high hopes for this foal, but the vet said the foal wouldn't have made it anyway."

"I'll go and see what I can do to help," Mr. McLean said, reaching for his jacket. "Everyone's going to be pretty tired this morning."

Samantha, after bolting down a glass of orange juice, followed him out to the yard.

Mike and Ashleigh were with Wonder. After talking to them, Samantha's father hurried off to help

Len, Mr. Reese, and Vic tend to the other horses, giving them their morning feed before leading them out to the pastures and mucking out the stalls. Wonder looked much better than she did the night before, but Ashleigh looked dead on her feet.

"I think she's going to be okay," Ashleigh said wearily.

"But you aren't going to be," Mike told her, "if you don't go in and get some sleep."

"You'll need my help out here."

"We'll manage," Samantha said.

"I have to wait for Mr. Townsend. I called him this morning, and he said he'd be right over."

Samantha heard the crunch of tires on gravel, and a moment later Mr. Townsend hurried into the barn, looking distraught. The news of the lost foal had to have come as a shock and disappointment to him, too.

He nodded a sad greeting, then looked into the stall at Wonder, as if to reassure himself of the mare's condition. He walked over and laid a hand on Wonder's neck. "She's doing all right?" he asked Ashleigh. "Has the vet been here this morning since I talked to you?"

"He should be here within an hour. Mike's father checked her over a little while ago and said that everything seems to be normal."

"That's a relief. Too often there's a problem with a miscarriage this late in term. You said the foal she lost was a colt?" Mr. Townsend asked.

Ashleigh nodded. "But undersize, with badly deformed forelegs. The vet said he wouldn't have made

131

it anyway. Dr. Mendez is going to do a more thorough examination and let us know what he finds."

Mr. Townsend expelled a long, sad breath. "What a terrible disappointment, especially since Wonder's already produced such outstanding offspring. This is a real blow coming right after Princess's injury."

"I know," Ashleigh said grimly.

At least things couldn't possibly get any worse, Samantha thought.

12

BY THE END OF THE NEXT WEEK WONDER WAS WELL enough to go out in the paddock with the other mares, most of whom, including Fleet Goddess, were heavy with foal. Wonder seemed lost, as if she was searching for her own missing foal. It broke Samantha's heart, but at least Wonder was on the mend, and she could have other foals.

On Friday, Ashleigh stopped Samantha as she came home from school. "I've made up my mind," Ashleigh said. "I've decided it's time I talked to Mr. Townsend about Pride. I'm going over this afternoon. Do you want to come with me and back me up?"

"Definitely!"

Still, Samantha felt her stomach flutter with nerves as they headed up the Townsend Acres drive. Clay Townsend was a very important person in the racing business. Samantha knew it wasn't going to be easy for Ashleigh to tell him she didn't agree with his decision.

They went to see Princess first. Hank led them to the big padded stall where Princess was housed. He had put up the padding to ensure that the filly didn't accidentally bang her injured leg against the wooden stall sides and do more damage.

"I was really sorry to hear about Wonder's foal," Hank said sadly. "You didn't need that now."

"No, we didn't," Ashleigh said, "but thanks, Hank."

"Princess seems to be coming along, anyway," Hank told Ashleigh. "I can't say she's fond of the cast, but she's putting up with it and doesn't seem to be in any pain. She's eating well, too."

"Did the vet give you any idea of when the cast can come off?" Samantha asked.

"Not for a month, I wouldn't imagine," Hank said. "He'll periodically X-ray her leg to see that the fracture's healing as it should. It's not easy keeping her quiet, though. She wants to be out and about, but she has plenty of company so she's not too bored. She's gotten to be one of the favorites of the staff. They're always stopping by to see how she's doing."

"What about Lavinia?" Samantha couldn't help asking.

"Lavinia hasn't set foot near her stall. Embarrassed, probably. Townsend Senior raised the roof when he found out Lavinia was riding."

They spent several more minutes at Princess's stall. The pretty chestnut filly had a sweet and trusting personality, despite the trauma she'd been through. She was very much like her mother, Samantha thought. What a shame it would be if she could never race.

"I'm on my way to talk to Mr. Townsend," Ashleigh said to Hank. "Do you know if he's around?"

"He was in his office a half-hour ago. Maybe it's none of my business," Hank said, "but are you going to talk to him about Pride's retirement?"

"Yup. Wish me luck."

"You've got it."

Samantha remembered another time when she and Ashleigh had confronted Mr. Townsend in his office— when Pride was a yearling, and Mr. Townsend had nearly been forced to sell his half-interest in the colt. It seemed so long ago now, but here they were, once again talking to Mr. Townsend about Pride's future.

Ashleigh knocked on the open office door. Mr. Townsend looked up from the papers on his desk and seemed surprised to see them.

"Do you have a few minutes, Mr. Townsend?" Ashleigh asked. "I'd like to talk to you."

"Yes. Come on in. Sit down." For an instant he frowned. "Nothing's wrong, I hope. Wonder—"

"She's fine," Ashleigh assured him. "I came to talk about Pride's retirement."

Mr. Townsend nodded. "We do need to talk."

"I've given it a lot of thought," Ashleigh said quickly, "and I'm against retiring him this year. I know the pros and cons—"

Mr. Townsend raised a hand, stopping her. *Oh, no*, Samantha thought. *He's not even going to listen.*

"I've been doing some thinking myself since I first talked to you about this," Mr. Townsend said. "And, of course, we've had two sad disappointments in the meantime. When I first considered retiring Pride, it was with the knowledge that Townsend Princess would be starting her two-year-old season. Hank, Maddock, and my son all thought she had the potential to be a quality racehorse. Now there's no guarantee she'll even race—and again I apologize to you for what happened, Ashleigh." He shifted in his chair a little uncomfortably as if he was blaming himself for Princess's injury. "But even before these last two disappointments," he continued, "I was reconsidering my decision about retiring Pride. You are right in saying there is no physical reason to cut short his career. He's fit, and this last season doesn't seem to have taken a toll on him. I do worry about injury, but I've begun to think that's taking the pessimistic viewpoint. Neither you nor I would run him if there was even the slightest possibility he wasn't one hundred percent fit. And I have to admit that I'd miss the excitement of his racing. From a purely business standpoint, Pride keeps Townsend Acres in the headlines. From a more sentimental standpoint, he's a joy to watch. I feel extremely proud knowing he was bred on this farm."

As she listened, Samantha felt a rising elation. The discussion wasn't going as she and Ashleigh had expected at all.

"I guess you see where all this is leading," Mr. Townsend said. "I agree with you that Pride should race another year. We'll keep our fingers crossed and hope that he performs as well as this past year. No matter what, I think he deserves the opportunity to show just how outstanding he is."

Samantha glanced over to Ashleigh and saw her joyous and almost disbelieving expression. "I'm so glad you've made this decision, Mr. Townsend. Thank you!"

Suddenly from outside the office a voice shrieked, "I don't believe it!"

Ashleigh and Samantha spun around to see Lavinia standing in the doorway. Obviously she'd overheard the conversation. Her face was flushed with anger. "How can you change your mind now? You're letting *her* get her way again? This is absolutely ridiculous. Sending Pride to stud is the only economically sensible thing to do! She only has a half-interest in Pride because of *your* generosity! Why should *she* have anything to say at all?"

"We'll discuss this later, Lavinia." There was a stern warning in Mr. Townsend's tone that surprised Samantha.

"But it's absurd. Isn't the fact that Wonder just lost her foal proof that they're not capable of giving the horses proper—" Lavinia stopped abruptly as her father-in-law's mouth tightened in anger. Lavinia turned and strode off, but not before giving Ashleigh a look of loathing.

Mr. Townsend was obviously not only angry but

embarrassed at Lavinia's outburst. *Maybe,* Samantha thought, *he isn't as taken in by her as everybody thinks.*

Ashleigh rose, trying to cover the uncomfortable moment. "I know you're busy," she said. "And Sammy and I have to get back to Whitebrook. But I really am so happy that you've decided to let Pride race another year. I know he'll live up to our expectations."

"I hope so, too, Ashleigh," Mr. Townsend said. He still seemed to be recovering from his daughter-in-law's outburst. "Please disregard what Lavinia said about Wonder. I know what good care she receives at Whitebrook. No one can be blamed for her miscarriage. It was just a misfortune. I'll stop by Whitebrook during the week," he added. "We can talk more then about a training and race schedule."

"Fine," Ashleigh said.

"Whew!" Samantha said as she and Ashleigh strode away from his office. "I can hardly believe it!"

"I'm almost afraid he'll change his mind," Ashleigh murmured as they headed back to Ashleigh's car.

"I know what you mean," Samantha said. "But it's such good news, Ash! Pride can keep racing!"

A smile spread over Ashleigh's face. "I didn't realize how nervous I was until now. I kept telling myself that I would convince him—but I always had doubts. It was easier than I ever dreamed! He's thinking the same way we are. Do you know what a relief that is?"

"Yes, I do," Samantha said. "I've been scared out of my mind that Pride would be retired and moved to Townsend Acres. And I can't believe he apologized for Lavinia. I sure wouldn't want to be in her shoes right now."

"Neither would I," Ashleigh said. "But she really went too far that time."

"Mr. Townsend was *not* happy. Maybe he'll finally lay down the law. I don't think he had any idea how controlling she got while he was away in England."

There was no sign of Lavinia anywhere in the stable yard. "It's been a really tough time, Sammy," Ashleigh said, "but maybe—finally—better days are ahead. I can't wait to tell Mike the good news! He'll be as thrilled as we are!"

Samantha knew Tor and Yvonne would be, too.

They were, of course. Tor hugged Samantha when she gave him the news that night. "That's great, Sammy! I'm so glad you finally got some good news. I know how hard it's been for you. Let's go out and celebrate."

Knowing that Pride would continue racing, Samantha finally began to feel in the Christmas spirit. As the December days grew colder she and Yvonne went Christmas shopping in Lexington after school. They all firmed up their plans for the Christmas show and party for the disabled students. And there was the big dance at school to look forward to and Samantha's seventeenth birthday a week before Christmas.

Now that they had Mr. Townsend's support, Ashleigh and Samantha forged ahead with plans for Pride's training and race schedule. "We haven't had a deep frost yet," Ashleigh said. "If the training oval stays in good condition, I thought we could start taking him out for a few slow gallops next week. We don't want him to get too fat and lazy lounging around the paddock."

Samantha smiled. Pride looked neither fat nor lazy. He had put on a few pounds, but he'd needed to. Taking him out for a few relaxed gallops would be a good idea, though. He would be in better shape when he went into intensive training in January.

"It's such a relief to have the retirement thing settled," Ashleigh said. "But I still have this dread that Mr. Townsend will change his mind again."

"I don't think he will," Samantha said. "I'd be more worried that Lavinia and Brad have something else up their sleeves."

"I asked Hank, but he hasn't heard any stable gossip. If Mr. Townsend said anything to Lavinia after her outburst, it was in private."

"And if he bawled her out, Lavinia isn't going to go around talking about it. I wonder what plans they have for Lord Ainsley now?"

"Hard to say," Ashleigh answered. "Rather than take the chance of losing to Pride again, they might avoid the races he's entered in."

"Then they'd have to skip some of the biggest races," Samantha said. "I can't see them doing that."

"Figuring out what they're up to is always a guessing game," Ashleigh said. "Except that you can usually count on it being unpleasant. How are you and Tor coming with your show?"

140

"Fine. Beth's been a big help, and Yvonne and I bought gifts for each of the kids. It'll be fairly simple—just enough to give them a chance to show off a little. Why don't you try to come? It's this weekend. Meeting Pride's half-owner and trainer would really give the kids a thrill, especially this one little girl, Mandy. She idolizes Pride, and she's really been working hard with her riding."

"Maybe I will," Ashleigh said with a smile. "I'd love to have a look at Tor's stable, too."

13

ON SATURDAY, TOR'S STABLE GROOMS GAVE THE PONIES A special grooming. They braided red and green ribbons into their manes and tails and gave their coats an extra brushing. Beth came to the stable early and helped set up a table of cookies and punch, and while Samantha and Yvonne made a last-minute inspection of the ring, Tor gave Ashleigh a tour of the stables.

"You've done a great job," Ashleigh said to Tor when they returned to the ring. "I can see why you're doing so well."

"What did you think of Top Hat?" Samantha asked.

"He's got a real jumper's build—incredible hindquarters," Ashleigh said. "Tor is lending me a video of his last show so I can see how he looks in action."

A few minutes later the children began arriving with their parents, siblings, and friends. They oohed with delight when they saw the ponies, then eyed the refreshment table and the small pile of gifts at one end. Janet and Beth made introductions, then directed the guests to the bleachers set up at one end of the indoor ring.

When everyone was settled and the children had been helped onto their ponies, Tor made a brief welcoming speech. "I want you to know how much we've enjoyed working with the children. Not only has it been fun, but it's been rewarding and inspiring for everyone involved, students *and* teachers. All our riders can be proud of what they have achieved over the past several weeks." The speech was met with smiles and a small round of applause. Then Tor turned to the students. "And we've got a treat for you guys—a special visitor has come to watch you ride. You all know who Wonder's Pride is. We talk about him a lot around here, and most of you saw him win the Breeders' Cup. Well, his co-owner and trainer, Ashleigh Griffen, is here today."

Ashleigh smiled and waved from the side of the ring, looking a little self-conscious as six pairs of eyes turned and stared at her.

"Oh, wow!" Mandy gasped with excitement. Samantha glanced over and saw that the little girl's eyes were sparkling. "Oh, but now I'm going to be *really* nervous!"

There was sympathetic laughter from the audience.

"You don't have to be," Ashleigh called over with a grin. "And after you've all finished, I'll be glad to talk to you and answer any questions you have about Pride and racing."

"All right!" one of the boys exclaimed.

"Let's get started, then," Tor said. "Timmy, you're first."

Samantha watched as the little boy moved his pony forward. During the weeks of classes each of the children had learned to ride without a training lead and to rein their ponies through simple figures at a walk and trot.

Timmy moved his pony around the ring with confidence. He smiled proudly when he brought his pony to a stop, faced the stands, and received a big round of applause.

Robert and Charmaine rode out and did equally well. Then it was Mandy's turn. Samantha gave her a smile of encouragement, although she had no doubt that Mandy would do a good job. Her lower legs were encumbered by braces, but she had a perfect, natural seat and light hands and could communicate with her mount. Just as important, she loved what she was doing and was always striving to improve.

When Mandy finished, Samantha gave her a thumbs-up, and the little girl seemed to glow.

After Jane and Aaron had demonstrated their newly acquired skills and, with big grins, received their share of applause, Tor congratulated all the students. "You all did a fantastic job! What do you say— do you think it's time to party?"

He was greeted by a chorus of yeses. They helped the children from their mounts, then Beth and Janet passed out the gifts to each of the children and were met with pleased smiles. "Oh, boy!"

Mandy said. "I didn't expect a present!"

The guests had come down from the bleachers and broke into groups as they praised the children and admired the ponies. Samantha saw that Ashleigh was soon surrounded by the students and their parents.

As Samantha collected a cookie from the table and looked out at all the smiling faces, Beth walked up to her.

"I'd say our show was a big success," Beth said happily. "You all have done a great job with these kids. I've been meaning to tell you, Sammy, what a good influence you've been on Mandy. Her parents spoke to me earlier. They said that since she started these lessons, her spirits have really lifted. All she talks about is you and riding, and she doesn't have nearly as many bouts of frustration and anger."

"I'm glad," Samantha said, blushing a little at Beth's praise. She looked over at Mandy, who was standing beside Ashleigh asking questions a mile a minute. "It's good to know we've been able to help."

Beth put an arm around Samantha's shoulders and gave her a gentle squeeze. "Thanks."

Early the following week Samantha took Pride out for a gallop on the training oval. Len had run the harrow over the track the day before, loosening up the surface, since Mike and Ian McLean still had a couple of horses in active training. After Christmas the horses would be shipped to Florida for the winter racing season.

Ashleigh watched from the rail as Pride stretched

out in a smooth, relaxed gallop. Samantha smiled with delight as she rode him through two circuits on the mile track. Pride hadn't even worked up a sweat when she rode him off the track, patting his neck affectionately.

Ashleigh grinned as she looked him over. "He's stayed in super condition. Did he feel as good as he looked?" she asked Samantha.

"He sure did. He felt great."

"Glad to be out there on the track again, boy?" Ashleigh asked the big horse as she rubbed his nose. Pride whickered and tossed his head so his silky mane shimmered. "If we don't get any ice or snow, we can try working him every other day," Ashleigh said. "Then after Christmas we'll get down to serious training. Speaking of Christmas, Mike and I are putting up our tree tonight. I'm so excited—our first Christmas together since we've been married!"

"I picked up some red ribbon after school yesterday. I could do the wreaths for the barns," Samantha offered eagerly.

"Go to it. I'm looking forward to Christmas a lot more than I thought I would a few weeks ago."

"So am I," Samantha agreed. "With Pride going back in training, it looks like it will be a pretty good Christmas after all."

"Your birthday's coming up, too, isn't it?" Ashleigh asked.

Samantha nodded. "On Sunday. Tor's taking me out to dinner at Le Château. And Saturday night is the Christmas dance at school."

Ashleigh lifted her brows. "Wow! Sounds like a busy weekend. And Le Château is a pretty romantic place."

Samantha's cheeks reddened at Ashleigh's knowing smile. "It was Tor's choice." She could hardly wait for her romantic birthday evening.

As Samantha had expected, they all had a wonderful time at the dance. She and Yvonne had shopped together for their dresses, and they were rewarded by compliments from Tor and Gregg, who both looked very handsome themselves. All the decorations and good company really put Samantha in the Christmas mood. When they left the dance to drive home, there were even a few snowflakes falling.

"Hey, great," Tor said. "Maybe we'll have a white Christmas."

Samantha laughed. "With a week still to go, don't you think you're jumping the gun? And how often do we have a white Christmas in Kentucky?"

"It would be fun, though."

"You're right there," Samantha said, leaning over to give him a kiss. When they got back to Whitebrook, she invited Tor to take a look at the barns she had decorated. "I think maybe I got carried away when we got the good news about Pride. I put wreaths all over the place, but the horses seem to like it."

They headed toward the stables. Even before Samantha opened the door to the training barn, she heard a terrible racket, like a cat yowling in distress. "One of the barn cats," she said to Tor. "I hope nothing's wrong."

"It's probably Sidney wanting to get out for a night on the town."

It was Sidney, but he didn't want to get out. When he saw them, he dashed off in the direction of Pride's stall, with his tail flared in alarm. Samantha and Tor hurried after him. Samantha now heard the groans and grunts of a horse in pain. *Not Pride!* she thought. But when they reached Pride's stall, to their horror, they found him down on his side, groaning and thrashing wildly with his legs.

"Oh, my God!" Samantha gasped. "It looks like colic. Get the others! We'll need to call the vet!"

Tor dashed off. Samantha entered the stall, careful to avoid Pride's thrashing legs. "It's me, boy," she called out softly. "I'm here." Pride answered with another grunt of pain. Samantha's heart was pounding in fear. She knew that colic could be deadly to a horse, especially if it wasn't caught in time—and if Pride was down in his stall, thrashing, he wasn't in the early stages. Horses couldn't regurgitate, so if anything toxic got into their system, upsetting their digestion, it was serious. Even overeating could cause colic, but that couldn't be the case with Pride. Samantha always carefully rationed his grain.

Mike and Ashleigh rushed into the barn. Len and Mr. McLean followed. "The vet's on his way," Mike said, taking in Pride's state. "It looks like severe colic all right," he said grimly. "We've got to try to get him up on his feet and walking. Otherwise, he might not get up at all!"

All of them worked frantically to get Pride up.

They had to avoid his thrashing legs. He was in such pain and distress, he didn't even seem to know them. Samantha cringed to think that her beloved horse might have been in pain for hours while she was out dancing.

"If it's colic, I can't imagine what could have caused it," Len said anxiously. "Our hay supply is fresh, and there aren't any weeds in the paddock he could have gotten into. All the other horses seem fine, though Mr. Reese and Vic are out double-checking them now."

At last they got Pride to his feet and coaxed him out into the aisle. Ashleigh and Samantha held either side of his halter and started him walking. They spoke soothingly to him, but he seemed beyond hearing their words. They exchanged a fear-filled glance. "I wish the vet would get here!" Ashleigh murmured in choked tones.

Walking didn't seem to ease Pride's distress, and when the vet finally hurried into the barn, Samantha was nearly beside herself with worry.

"How long has he been like this?" Dr. Mendez asked as he examined Pride.

"We don't know," Ashleigh told him. "Sammy and Tor found him like this about a half-hour ago."

"I don't like the looks of it," the vet said. "His temperature is way up. This could be more than colic—possibly an intestinal blockage, but I can't determine that here. I want you to van him right over to the hospital. I'll call up my assistant and meet you there. And whatever you do, keep him on his feet!"

Samantha felt a cold chill of dread. Her father and Mike rushed out to ready the smaller of the vans. Samantha, Ashleigh, Tor, and Len quickly bandaged Pride's legs for the journey, then led him into the pre-dawn darkness.

Mike pushed the van to its fastest safe speed as they rushed Pride into Lexington. The others stayed in the back with Pride, supporting him and trying to comfort him, but it was all they could do to keep him standing. Samantha felt the warm wetness of tears streaming down her cheeks. Tor looked over with barely disguised fear in his own eyes. He reached for her hand and held it tightly.

When Mike pulled to a stop by the big rear doors of the hospital, Dr. Mendez and one of his assistants hurried out to help. Between them, they backed Pride off the van and got him inside.

Pride was taken off to the examination room. One of the veterinary staff led them to the vet's office, where they could wait. Ashleigh was white faced. "This can't be happening. I'm scared."

"So am I," Samantha whispered.

"And just when we thought everything was going so well."

14

AS THE MINUTES TICKED BY, SAMANTHA BURIED HER FACE in her hands, wondering what was going on in the examination room. Not knowing only increased her fears. Tor sat beside her on the couch in the vet's office. Ashleigh stood at the window and gazed out unseeingly into the darkness beyond. Mike sat on one of the side chairs. His brow was furrowed with worry. Ashleigh had called Mr. Townsend with the terrible news, and he looked tired and disheveled when he arrived. He spoke quietly with Ashleigh as they continued to wait.

When Dr. Mendez finally appeared, his news was worse than they had expected. "He has a twisted intestine," the vet said without preamble. "He'll require immediate surgery if we're to save him. I need your permission to proceed."

"Yes, of course," Ashleigh and Mr. Townsend said without hesitation.

"I want to forewarn you," the vet continued, "even if the surgery is successful, it will still be touch and go. The intestine may already have ruptured and poisons may already be in his system. That, of course, could cause complications from infection."

"So this is definitely life threatening," Mr. Townsend said somberly.

"I'm afraid it is," the vet confirmed.

"Just do whatever you can to save him," Ashleigh said desperately. "Pride is so very, very special!"

"I'm well aware of that, and of course I'll do everything I can. You can wait here if you like. It may be a long procedure. One of the staff will bring you coffee." He hurried off.

Samantha again dropped her head into her hands. *Oh, Pride,* she thought, *please be all right . . . please. I couldn't stand to lose you, too. There's been too much death . . . Charlie, and Wonder's foal . . . please pull through!* Hot tears trickled down her cheeks, but she was too numb to feel them.

Tor put his arm around her shoulders and spoke softly. "I'm sorry, Sammy. It's just one bad thing after another. I wish there was something I could do to make it easier for you."

"I know," Samantha whispered hoarsely, feeling his concern for her. She looked up and their eyes locked.

"We'll get through this," Tor murmured. "Somehow."

The wait seemed endless. One of the staff brought them coffee and doughnuts, but no one had any interest in eating.

Samantha checked her watch—four in the morning, and neither she nor Tor had even been to bed. She felt dizzy from worry and lack of sleep when the vet returned to the office with his report.

"The good news is that he's come through the surgery," he said. Samantha reached over and took Tor's hand. He squeezed it warmly in return.

"Unfortunately," Dr. Mendez continued, "the intestine had ruptured. I've repaired the damage. We had to remove a small section of the intestine, but that's not the problem. The problem is that poisons were in his system and infection had already set in. He's a very sick animal. I can't give you any guarantees that he'll pull through."

Samantha tried to choke back her tears. She saw Ashleigh close her eyes in pain. Mr. Townsend looked drained and shook his head sadly. Who could have imagined that less than two months after Pride's impressive victory in the Breeders' Cup, he would be near death?

"Can we see him?" Samantha asked.

"He's still recovering from the anesthesia," the vet said. "Maybe in a couple of hours. I'm really sorry to be the bearer of such unhopeful tidings."

Since there was nothing they could do at the hospital, they all returned to Whitebrook. It was nearly five in the morning. Samantha had had no sleep at all, but she knew sleep was impossible until she could see Pride. She showered and changed. Tor waited downstairs and talked to her father, then showered himself. It all seemed so unreal. Only two days before she had galloped Pride on the oval. He'd been so fit, so full of life, and she and Ashleigh had both been looking forward to the year ahead with excited optimism. How could everything have changed so quickly and so drastically?

Samantha, Tor, and Mr. McLean sat around the kitchen table, talking quietly. "Pride was in perfect physical condition before this," Mr. McLean said, trying to buoy Samantha's spirits. "That will help him now."

"But the vet sounded so pessimistic," Samantha said, again fighting back tears.

"He has to prepare you for all possibilities," her father reassured her. "That doesn't mean he's expecting the worst to happen."

"I know, but Dad, Pride was so sick! I've never seen a horse in so much pain!"

"I'm just glad we found him when we did," Tor said quietly. "Though now I wish we'd gotten back from the dance a couple of hours sooner."

"So do I," Samantha said miserably.

Three hours later Dr. Mendez called to say that they could see Pride, but not to expect too much. Samantha was glad she had been forewarned, because Pride was in a worse state than she'd expected. His normally bright eyes were dull, and he was almost completely unresponsive to her and Ashleigh's presence.

"Is he in pain?" Samantha asked.

The vet shook his head. "We've given him something. Right now he's still feeling the aftereffects of the anesthetic, and his system is doing battle trying to overcome the infection. I've got him on antibiotics, and we'll keep a close eye on him. When he seems more stable, we'll move him to one of the hospital stalls."

Samantha saw from the vet's eyes that he didn't want to raise their expectations. They stayed for another hour, talking to Pride and stroking his neck, but there was little change in his listless condition.

"We'll hope for more improvement tomorrow," the vet told them as they prepared to leave. "Someone will call you if there's any change."

Samantha dropped a gentle kiss on Pride's nose. "Get better, boy," she whispered urgently. "Please!" Pride didn't respond at all, not even by a flick of his ears. Samantha felt totally drained and depressed as they walked out to the car.

"I know we were supposed to go out for my birthday tonight," Samantha said to Tor as Mike drove back to Whitebrook. "Would you mind if we didn't go? I'm not in any shape. I couldn't even pretend to have a good time."

"Not a very good birthday for you, is it?" Tor said sadly. "Of course I don't mind canceling. We'll go out another time when we feel like celebrating. Probably the best thing for both of us is to get a good night's sleep. The next few days are going to be pretty stressful."

Samantha knew just how stressful they would be, especially if Pride made no improvement.

*   *   *

157

By the following morning Pride had been moved to a roomy stall in the stabling wing of the facilities, where he was checked frequently by one of the veterinary assistants. There was little change in his condition. His eyes were a little less dull, and he responded with a flick of his ears to her and Ashleigh's voices, but it was obvious the beautiful horse was miserable.

Over the next days Samantha and Ashleigh alternated their time with Pride. Fortunately school vacation had begun. They spent hours sitting in his stall, talking softly to him, massaging him, trying to get him to eat the light diet provided for him. The vet told them frankly that Pride's lack of appetite wasn't a good sign.

As word of Pride's illness spread around the racing industry, dozens of concerned calls came in to Whitebrook. Mr. Townsend offered to put together a press release, since none of them was prepared to deal with constant calls.

Neither Ashleigh nor Samantha was about to give up hope, but as the days slowly passed with no improvement, it was growing increasingly difficult to feel optimistic. Pride seemed to want to respond, but he was simply much too ill.

All Samantha's friends were supportive. Tor came with her to the hospital as often as he could. Yvonne and Maureen called daily to see how Pride was doing and to try to boost Samantha's spirits. Her father and Beth were there for her, too, but Samantha wasn't alone in feeling the strain and worry. Everyone at

Whitebrook was affected. Len went about his tasks with a heavy heart.

"I can't believe that big guy's so sick," he told Samantha. "Here he was galloping around the oval like a champ two days before, and when I checked him that night, he was fine. I would have noticed something wrong."

"It's not your fault, Len," Samantha assured him.

"Yeah, I know. Ashleigh and Mike have told me the same. I still can't help feeling responsible. It's just real fortunate that you and Tor stopped in the barn when you did." Len didn't have to add that Pride wouldn't have made it through the night if they hadn't found him then.

But by late Thursday, when Samantha visited the hospital, Pride had still shown no real improvement, and Samantha was beginning to feel desperate. The thought that Pride might die was more than she could stand.

"We love you," she whispered to him. "I don't know what I'd do without you. You've always had so much heart and courage. I know you can fight this, Pride, and get better!"

Pride gave the softest of nickers in response, but even that seemed to take all his strength.

On Christmas Day they all gathered at Ashleigh and Mike's. The tree was decorated and covered in lights, and there was a pile of presents beneath its branches, but no one could feel much joy. Pride wasn't any better. The night before they'd followed their usual tradition by bringing midnight treats to all the horses in the barn. That morning Samantha and Tor had taken special treats to Pride, but he hadn't been tempted. He'd turned his head away.

"Mr. Townsend called earlier," Ashleigh said as they sat in the Reese living room. A fire was blazing on the hearth, but the dancing flames brought no coziness or cheer. "He had just been over to see Pride. I know he's trying to keep up his hopes, but he sounded pretty depressed. He said he thinks we should both talk to the vet tomorrow."

"About what?" Samantha asked in alarm.

"He didn't say, but I suppose he's thinking that Pride might not make it. He's not getting any better. He's getting worse." Suddenly Ashleigh covered her face with her hands and burst into tears. Mike tried to comfort her, but there really wasn't anything he could say. It didn't look good.

"He *has* to get better," Samantha murmured to Tor. "If we keep letting him know we're there for him, I just can't believe he won't improve."

Tor didn't say anything. Samantha guessed it was because he and Mike both thought that Mr. Townsend was going to suggest having Pride put down.

I'm not giving up! Samantha thought. *Pride can't die!*

The next morning she drove into Lexington with Ashleigh. Mr. Townsend would meet them at the hospital. As Samantha approached Pride's stall she prayed she would see an improvement—that Pride would prick his ears and nicker a welcome to her. He didn't. He seemed grateful when she caressed his ears and rubbed her hands over his back, but Samantha could see how much weight he had lost. Each of his ribs showed clearly, and his brilliant copper coat had lost its shine. He would starve to death if he didn't start eating soon.

"Oh, fella," she said, resting her forehead against his neck and realizing the truth she didn't want to believe. Her beloved horse was going downhill fast. "Give it one more shot, please! I know it's not easy when you're so sick, but don't give up yet! You've got too many great years ahead of you."

She continued resting her forehead against Pride's warm neck, feeling a growing sense of desolation. She heard quiet voices and footsteps approaching the stall and turned as Ashleigh and Mr. Townsend entered with the vet.

He gave Samantha a sympathetic look. She knew that tears stained her cheeks. "As you can see for yourselves," he said quietly to Ashleigh and Mr. Townsend, "he's gotten worse in the last twenty-four hours. He's not responding to the antibiotics. His temperature is still too high; he refuses to eat. I'm afraid there's been too much stress on his system and he can't fight back anymore." Dr. Mendez paused. "I know it's a heart-wrenching decision to make, but if he hasn't shown any improvement by morning, the only humane thing to do is put him down. I know he's an incredibly valuable animal and he's obviously loved, but he's suffering."

Samantha stared at the vet. "No! You can't. You can't!"

"It's not my decision to make," Dr. Mendez said kindly. "I'm just giving you my opinion of what I think is the compassionate course."

Ashleigh and Mr. Townsend looked as stunned and horrified as Samantha felt.

"I'd hoped it wouldn't come to this," Mr. Townsend said. "You honestly don't hold out any hope for him?"

"Sorry, but no—short of a miracle. He's too weak. I can't see him rebounding now."

Mr. Townsend took a deep breath and stared into space. "I've had to make a decision like this before. It's never easy."

"No, it isn't, especially with a horse like this."

There were several moments of dead silence. Ashleigh's face was stricken. Mr. Townsend stared off in private and unhappy thought. Samantha wrapped her arms around Pride's neck and held him as if by will alone she could change what was happening.

"I can't do it!" Ashleigh's voice trembled. "I can't make that decision. Not Pride. Not yet!"

"I know how you feel, Ashleigh," Mr. Townsend said. "I hate to think of putting him down. But we have to think of Pride. He's suffering, and if he doesn't improve by tomorrow, I don't see how we can hold out any hope. His condition will only continue deteriorating . . . he'll suffer all the more."

15

TEARS STREAMED DOWN SAMANTHA'S CHEEKS AS SHE heard Ashleigh respond brokenly to Mr. Townsend. "I don't want him to suffer either. But can we please wait until morning to make the final decision? I want him to have every possible chance."

"As do I," Mr. Townsend said. "In the meantime, let's pray for a miracle."

Samantha couldn't bear to leave Pride. These might be the last hours she had to spend with him. She called Tor and could barely get the words out as she described the situation.

"He only has until morning . . . if he doesn't improve . . ."

"I'll be over as soon as I finish my last class," Tor said. "Call me if anything happens."

"I will."

"I'll be thinking of you. Hang in there, Sammy."

Samantha and Ashleigh both stayed at the clinic

for the rest of the day. They took turns rubbing Pride down and trying to coax him to eat. They talked to him. Nothing seemed to work. Late in the afternoon when Ashleigh suggested they go home for a while, Samantha shook her head.

"I'm not leaving him tonight. He needs someone here with him."

"You can't stay alone, Sammy. I mean, if—"

"Tor's coming. He'll be here in a little while."

"All right . . . I'll be back later. Sammy, I hate to say it . . . I hate to believe it's possible, but I don't think he's going to make it. I feel like I'm living in some kind of a nightmare." Ashleigh swallowed hard and blinked.

"I feel the same way. I want to pinch myself and wake up and find it's all been a bad dream."

"It hasn't been, though. Oh, God, let me get out of here before I totally break down. Sammy, I'll see you later."

Samantha watched Ashleigh rush off, knowing that Ashleigh was desperately trying to fight her tears and stay in control. Samantha returned to Pride's side and gently took his muzzle in her hands.

"Pride, please, *please* try to fight back. You can do it, boy. You *have* to. You don't have much time. If only there was some way I could help you!"

Pride looked back at her with his warm brown eyes. Was there a flicker of understanding in his gaze? Samantha wondered. Did he know how little time he had left? Was he too weak to care?

Samantha pressed her forehead to his. "Please

don't die," she murmured. "Try to find the will to live again."

"Sammy!"

She looked up as Tor entered the stall. He quickly stepped over and wrapped his arms around her. "I'm sorry . . . so, so sorry."

"It's not over yet," she said hoarsely. "I haven't given up hope."

Tor continued holding her for several minutes. "I brought you something to eat."

"I'm not hungry."

"You're not going to do Pride any good if you fall apart."

"I suppose not," Samantha said wearily, "but right now everything would taste like sawdust."

"I brought some soup from that deli near the stable. You love their food."

There was a quiet knock on the outside of the stall. They looked over. It was one of the veterinary assistants.

"Sorry," she said, "I know how you're both feeling. I don't want to interrupt, but I just want to check his vitals."

Samantha and Tor stepped apart as the assistant made a quick examination.

"Is his temperature down at all?" Samantha asked, unable to keep a wistful hope from her voice.

The assistant sadly shook her head. "No . . . I'm sorry to say it's not." She hesitated. "You're going to stay with him?"

"Yes."

"I'm on night duty. If you need me for anything,

I'll be in the office in the main complex. I'll hope for the best."

"Thanks," Samantha said.

The assistant continued down the row of stalls to check on the two other occupants of the wing.

Samantha managed to eat some of the soup. She called her father to tell him she was staying with Pride.

"Ashleigh told me," he said, "but Sammy, do you really think that's a good idea? It could only make you feel worse. Sometimes it's better just to accept the inevitable—as hurtful as it may be."

"I couldn't feel much worse, Dad. I know Pride may not make it through the night, and even if he does, tomorrow could be his last morning. I want to be with him. I don't want him to be alone. He's not just a horse, Dad. He's got more heart and personality than a lot of people do."

"I know, Sammy. You don't have to tell me."

When Samantha returned to the stall, she gave Pride another back rub, then stretched each of his legs to ease the tension in his muscles. Pride whuffed out a long breath, and Samantha's spirits immediately rose.

"I'm sure he's more alert, Tor," she said with desperation. "His eyes seem brighter. He's holding his head higher."

Tor shook his head sadly and came to her side. "Sammy, he's no better. I know how much you want to pretend he is, but he's still suffering. You know there was no change when the vet's assistant checked him." Tor put his arm around her shoulders and rested his cheek against her hair. "Come on and sit down before

166

you collapse. You've done everything you could for him. All we can do is keep him company now."

As she and Tor settled on the straw at the side of the stall, Samantha had all she could do to fight back the sobs that threatened to bubble up in her throat. She felt so choked up, she could hardly breathe as she gazed at Pride and remembered all their wonderful times together—the days caring for him when he was only a promising yearling; the hours they'd spent on the training oval, at the racetrack, and in the walking ring; the brilliant races he'd won and the cheering crowds. Even the disappointments of the races that were lost when the Townsends pressured him were memories she wanted to cherish. Most of all, though, she thought of the heart and courage Pride had always demonstrated and his sweet and loving personality. How she would miss him!

Finally the sobs overwhelmed her. She buried her face against Tor's shoulder and let them come.

"Sammy," Tor whispered worriedly. "Let me take you home. You're only tearing yourself apart by staying here."

Samantha stubbornly shook her head. "No, I am not leaving him. I'm not going to let him spend the last hours of his life alone! Would you leave Top Hat?".

"No," Tor said softly. "No, I wouldn't."

A few minutes later Pride folded his legs beneath him and, with a grunt, lay down on the bedding beside them. He seemed to have lost even the will to stand upright. Samantha cradled his head, and he let out a soft sigh. He closed his eyes as Samantha gently rubbed his ears and neck. "We're here for you, boy," she said softly. "We're here for you." She thought she heard Pride's barely audible answering whicker, but it could just as easily have been her imagination.

Samantha would rather Pride died in his sleep with her beside him than to have him face a lethal injection in the morning. She knew that death from the injection would come painlessly. Pride would simply close his eyes and fall into an everlasting sleep, but she knew she couldn't bear to watch.

From the warm expelled breaths Samantha felt on her hand, she knew Pride was only sleeping now. Her eyes wet with tears, she laid her head on Tor's shoulder and felt the comfort of his arm around her. She fought to keep her own eyes from closing—tonight of all nights she must stay awake—but her eyes were so heavy from misery and lack of sleep. She'd rest them for just a minute, she thought.

When she struggled up to alertness again, she felt groggy and stunned. Through sleep-clogged eyes she saw two windows that were bright with morning light. But there were no windows that size in the stall. She turned her head and saw a desk and chairs, bookcases, and framed diplomas on the walls. In the next instant her mind cleared, and she sat up with a jolt. She recognized her surroundings. She was in Dr. Mendez's office, but how had she gotten here? Tor must have moved her. Why couldn't she remember being moved? And why had he moved her in the first place?

Her heart suddenly contracted in fear. Something

had happened. Pride! Had he died? Had Tor moved her so that she wouldn't see his lifeless body?

Someone had covered her with a blanket. She threw it off and swung her legs over the edge of the couch. Her feeling of panic increased. It was morning. They were making the decision to put Pride down that morning . . . if he hadn't already died during the night. Samantha jumped up so quickly her head spun, and she had to steady herself for a moment. She couldn't believe Tor would do this to her! Her thoughts were in a frightened jumble as she made her way to the door, opened it, and stood for a second gazing out at the hallway. She looked across to the door of the stabling wing, then hurried toward it. Pushing through, Samantha saw Tor, Mike, Ashleigh, and Mr. Townsend standing outside Pride's stall.

They turned and saw her, and Tor rushed to meet her. "Why did you put me in there?" Samantha demanded, her tone angry from fear. "What's happened?"

Samantha could see the circles under Ashleigh's eyes. Ashleigh didn't look like she'd slept. She looked like she'd been crying.

"Pride's dead!" Samantha cried. "He died and you took me away!" Samantha was so beside herself with grief that she barely listened to Tor's words as he took her shoulders.

"He's not dead," Tor said. "I brought you to the vet's office after you fell asleep. I was so sure Pride would die during the night . . . I didn't want you to wake up to it."

"That's my decision to make—not yours! You

shouldn't have taken me away. I wanted to be with him!"

"Sammy, Sammy, listen!" Tor raised his voice to get through to her. "Pride didn't die."

Samantha looked over to the stall again. Inside she could see the heads of Dr. Mendez and one of his assistants. They were going to give Pride the injection that would end his life! No, she had to stop them. She at least had to see Pride one last time! Samantha wrenched herself out of Tor's grasp. "No! Don't kill him!" she shouted to the vet and his assistant.

Tor rushed after her. "Sammy, it's not what you think!"

"At least let me be with him!" Samantha cried, too upset to listen to Tor. She ran toward the stall opening. Tor caught up with her.

"Sammy, please listen to me! After I took you to the vet's office, I fell asleep, too. When I woke up, *Pride was on his feet!* He was at his feed trough. He was trying to eat. He nickered to me. Sammy, do you hear what I'm saying?"

For a moment, Samantha could only stare at him. Her brain could barely absorb the meaning of his words. Pride was better? "But Ashleigh's been crying!" Samantha said.

"Tears of happiness, Sammy," Ashleigh told her quickly.

Samantha took another step forward and could see inside the stall. Pride was standing near the back. He certainly didn't look the picture of health, but his head was up, his ears were pricked, and when he saw her, he nickered happily.

Samantha stared. She turned to Ashleigh, Mike, and Tor, and each of them smiled. Then she looked back to Pride and saw Dr. Mendez's encouraging smile, too.

"He's really better?" she asked, her voice shaking.

"He is," Dr. Mendez answered. "I found it almost impossible to believe when they told me this morning, but he has definitely made an overnight improvement."

"Oh, Pride!" Samantha rushed forward and threw her arms around his neck. "You did it—you did it. You wouldn't give up, would you?" Pride craned his neck around and rubbed his head against her shoulder. Samantha could tell he was still extremely weak, but this was the most response he'd shown since his illness.

"He's not out of the woods yet," Dr. Mendez said, as if trying to temper Samantha's excitement. "He's still got a long way to go before he's fully recovered."

Samantha turned to the vet. "But he's over the hump?"

Dr. Mendez nodded. "I'd say he's over the hump—unless there's a relapse. I've just given him a thorough examination. His temperature is down to close to normal. He finally seems to be winning the battle against the infection. I'll know more when I analyze the blood samples I've just taken."

With the vet's examination over, Ashleigh hurried into the stall to join Samantha. She gave Pride her own loving and relieved hug. "I was so afraid for you, big guy," she said.

"What could account for the sudden turnaround?" Mr. Townsend asked. "I couldn't be more delighted, but is it normal?"

The vet wagged his head. "I don't know." He looked over at Pride. "The antibiotics might finally have beaten the infection, but with an animal so weak, that's unusual. All I can say is that I've rarely seen a horse with such a will to live." There was a bemused look on his face as he studied Pride. "I'd almost say that he knew we'd inflicted a humanitarian death sentence on him and responded by recovering. Of course, that sounds like a pretty mystical explanation."

Samantha didn't think so.

Dr. Mendez fingered his chin. "There *are* accounts of horses seeming to read the human mind, responding to our thoughts and intentions with an extra sense. They can certainly sense danger in the wild, beyond the use of the normal senses."

"Pride's always seemed to understand us, as if he was reading our minds," Ashleigh murmured. "It's been such a horrible week. I'm so glad it's over. I couldn't sleep last night. When Mike and I got here early this morning, all I could think was the worst."

"We all thought that," Mr. Townsend said with a catch in his voice. "The prospect of putting Pride down was staggering to me, even when I thought there was no humane alternative."

"There's one other thing that might have helped Pride rebound," Tor said. "I'm surprised no one else has considered it. Love. I was with Sammy last night. I listened to her talking to Pride, encouraging him, asking him to find the will to live. And I know Ashleigh's done the same. Pride had to have felt all

172

that caring and concern. Maybe it gave him the extra courage and will to fight back."

Ashleigh smiled and looked over at Samantha.

"It could very well be," Dr. Mendez said. "Yesterday, I thought it would take nothing short of a miracle for him to recover."

"Then perhaps we've seen a miracle," Mr. Townsend said. "Whatever, he's on his way back. For that I'll be forever grateful!"

16

SAMANTHA WAS WEAK WITH RELIEF WHEN THEY LEFT THE clinic early that afternoon. Pride's condition remained stable. Although the vet had told them it was too soon to rule out a relapse, Pride's temperature remained down. He continued trying to eat the specially prepared feed the clinic had provided. Dr. Mendez reported that that morning's blood tests were encouraging. The infection was leaving Pride's bloodstream, but again he warned them all not to expect too much too soon. There was still an infection in Pride's system, and he would need to regain the considerable amount of weight he had lost during his illness before the vet would consider letting him leave the hospital. Still, compared to the way things had stood twelve hours before, it was wonderful news.

Samantha knew that if Pride had died, it would have been like a death in the family. He was that special to her. It had taken her so long to recover from the death of her mother, and she still hadn't gotten over her grief at Charlie's death. Losing Pride would really have been more than she could take.

As they drove back to Whitebrook in Mike's car, Tor suddenly cast Samantha a worried look. "Are you all right, Sammy?" he asked with alarm. "You're shaking like a leaf!"

Samantha looked down and realized her hands were trembling uncontrollably. "I think I'm shaking because it's over . . . because I'm so relieved. It's been so hard holding it all together this week."

Ashleigh looked over the seat with a smile. "You're not the only one who's feeling shaky, Sammy. So am I."

Tor put his arm around Samantha's shoulders. "You're sure you're not cold?"

"No . . . just very, very happy!"

So was everyone at Whitebrook when they got home. Ashleigh had called earlier to give everyone the good news, and now they rushed out into the drive. Samantha's father and Beth hugged her. Samantha was surprised to see Beth had tears in her eyes.

"Your father and I have been so worried about you," Beth said softly. "I know how much Pride means to you. You didn't deserve to have this happen. But I'm so glad Pride's better!"

"Thank you," Samantha responded, feeling truly touched by Beth's concern.

"You and I have gone through some tough patches," Beth added quietly, "not recently, but in the past. I hope those are over."

"Yes," Samantha assured her. "They're over." And Samantha really meant it.

Len stepped over with a wide grin cracking his face. He literally lifted Samantha off the ground in his exuberance. "You did it, little lady! You pulled him through!"

"He pulled himself through, Len," Samantha said, laughing.

"Sure, but not without your and Ashleigh's help. It was all that love you gave him. It made him want to keep on living. I'm proud of what you've done—Charlie would be, too. Though I have to admit I went through some pretty tough days there!"

"I guess we all did," Samantha said. She glanced around the stable yard at all the happy faces. Suddenly everything seemed sharper and clearer to her eyes. She realized that for more than a week she'd been walking around in a misty daze on automatic pilot, too concerned about Pride to react to anything else around her.

"I've made some sandwiches," Beth said to everyone. "Now that the worst of Pride's ordeal is over, maybe you'll all have some interest in eating again."

That brought a wave of laughter. Everyone filed up to the McLean cottage, where Beth had set out a veritable feast on the kitchen table—all of it nutritionally balanced, of course. Samantha had gotten used to Beth's insistence on healthy foods and had to admit she had even learned something from the older woman.

After everyone had eaten their fill, Samantha felt

exhaustion hit her like a hammer between the eyes. She could see that Tor, Ashleigh, and Mike felt the same. The tension and sleepless nights had caught up with them all.

Tor sat down on the couch next to Samantha and gave her a kiss on the cheek. "I'm going to head home before I fall down on the floor. You should try to get some sleep, too."

Samantha tried to smother a yawn. "I'm going to."

"I'll call you tonight. I guess you'll want to make a quick visit to Pride."

"Yes," Samantha responded, yawning again.

Tor smiled. "Sleep tight. I know I will."

When the others had left the cottage, Samantha climbed the stairs to her room. Her bed looked so inviting. *Oh, Pride,* she thought, *you're going to be all right!* Without even taking off her clothes, she flung herself down on the mattress and was out like a light.

Samantha, Tor, and Ashleigh visited Pride that night and twice the next day. Samantha was a little dismayed at his very slow improvement, but at least there were still no signs of relapse.

"Patience," Dr. Mendez told them when he stopped by the stall. "I know how you're all feeling, but you're not going to notice a startling transformation. It will take time for him to regain full health. He's been through a lot. Take heart in the fact that he's heading in the right direction now."

"You're sure?" Samantha asked. "You're not saying that just to make us feel better?"

The vet smiled. "I'm sure. I would never go around raising false hopes."

As the old year drew to a close, there seemed to be reason to hope. Samantha and Tor spent a quiet New Year's Eve together. After having dinner at the McLeans', they went to the clinic with Ashleigh and Mike to celebrate the coming of the New Year with Pride. Mike and Ashleigh had brought along a big thermos of hot apple cider, and they all toasted Pride and his continuing return to health. Pride took a curious whiff of the bubbly liquid and promptly pulled up his lip and snorted.

"We've brought something else for you, big guy," Samantha told him with a grin. She'd put together a basket filled with his favorite treats—carrots, apples, and even a couple of brown sugar cubes.

Tor looked at the cubes and raised his eyebrows. "Sugar? You think Dr. Mendez would approve?"

"It's natural, unprocessed sugar," Samantha said defensively. "Even Beth uses it. Pride deserves something extra special."

Tor laughed. "Just teasing, Sammy. I think he deserves something special, too."

Samantha returned to school two days later. She had of course kept in constant touch with Yvonne and Maureen during Pride's slow recovery. But she was stunned when she walked through the school door at the crowd of kids that suddenly rushed up to her with a barrage of questions.

"Pride's going to be all right?" "The papers said he might not make it." "He's going to, though, isn't he?"

179

Samantha stood in a daze, trying to take it all in and reassure everyone. "Yes, he's going to be okay. He keeps improving. It'll be a long while before he's back at Whitebrook, though."

"You must have been so afraid."

"I was," Samantha admitted as others came over to her voicing their concern. During Pride's illness, she'd been in her own little world. She hadn't really understood what his near death had meant to others.

"He probably won't race again, though," a girl from Samantha's trig class said with disappointment.

"I don't know. We haven't thought that far ahead."

Yvonne suddenly pushed through the crowd to rescue Samantha. "Come on, guys," she said. "I know you all love Pride, but give Sammy a break!"

There were a few embarrassed giggles in the crowd.

"Besides, the late bell is going to ring any second," Yvonne added.

"Oh, gosh . . . right," voices murmured. "Glad he's okay, Sammy!"

"Wow!" Samantha said as Yvonne ushered her off to their lockers. "I don't believe it!"

"You'd better. You don't know how many people have been asking me about you and Pride."

"It's great," Samantha said, still dazed. "I mean, it makes me feel good to know people care that much. I just wasn't expecting it."

Maureen hurried up with a grin on her pixie face. "Oh, Sammy, I'm glad to see you back! I'm so happy Pride's better. You're definitely going to have to write an article about what you went through—real human interest!"

Yvonne shook her head at Samantha. "Always the reporter, isn't she?" she said teasingly.

"Editor, Yvonne!" Maureen corrected. "And someday I'm going to be editor of more than the school newspaper."

"We know," Yvonne and Samantha said, exchanging a smile.

"Would you rather I wrote about Pride's illness or about our riding class for the disabled children?" Samantha asked with a twinkle in her eye.

"Oh, both. Definitely both!" Maureen said seriously. "I'll schedule Pride's story for this month and the riding class for next."

"Looks like you're going to be busy," Yvonne said to Samantha.

By the end of the week Pride was eating a regular diet and beginning to put on weight, although it would be a long time before he was back to normal. Still, Samantha was thrilled to see the shine returning to his coat and the hollows between his ribs slowly filling in. Dr. Mendez told them that Pride seemed to have totally kicked the infection. "Today's blood tests look very good. I'm going to be writing about *this* recovery for one of the veterinary journals," he smilingly told Ashleigh and Samantha.

Now that the worst seemed over, they started thinking of Pride's future again. Ashleigh, Mike, Samantha, and Tor talked about it one night after they'd returned to Whitebrook from the clinic.

"As much as we both wanted to see him keep racing," Ashleigh said to Samantha, "I don't think it's a possibility now."

"No," Samantha agreed. "He's been through too much. The only important thing now is that he's going to be okay."

"I think retiring him is the only decision you can make, Ash," Mike told her.

Ashleigh nodded.

"Have you talked to Mr. Townsend?" Samantha asked.

"No. Not yet. I don't think either of us has been thinking about whether he'd race again—only whether he'd live."

"I know," Samantha said. She remembered too well how unimportant another year of racing had seemed when Pride's whole life was at stake.

"But do you think Mr. Townsend will still want him sent to Townsend Acres for stud?" Tor asked.

Samantha shuddered. "I don't know if I could handle that. Lavinia and Brad haven't even called you, Ashleigh, since Pride got sick. They could at least have the decency to say they were sorry about Pride and wish you well. To have Pride over there anywhere near them would be awful!"

"It may not come to that," Tor said.

Ashleigh frowned. "No, it won't. When Pride's ready to leave the hospital, he's coming to Whitebrook. Mr. Townsend has really been shaken by what's happened. I think he's going to agree."

"If he gives you a hard time," Mike said, "I'll go with you and talk to him. We have really decent breeding facilities here. Townsend Acres would have nothing to lose by letting Pride stand here."

"Except the prestige of having Pride in their barn," Ashleigh reminded him.

"Before we start worrying, let's just pray for Pride to get totally back on his feet. I'm sure that's Clay Townsend's main concern, too."

The next morning, three weeks after Samantha thought she had lost Pride forever, she, Ashleigh, and Tor drove out to the hospital to find Mr. Townsend already standing outside Pride's stall, looking over the half-door. He turned and smiled when he saw them.

"What an improvement!" he said. "I almost can't believe it! He's eating like a champ today."

How things had changed in two weeks, Samantha thought. Pride gave a joyous, welcoming whinny and stepped quickly over to the stall door to greet her and Ashleigh. Samantha laughed with delight when he thrust his soft muzzle at both of them and blew out sweet-scented breaths as they rubbed his ears.

"Oh, big guy," Samantha said happily. "You really are getting better. And look at you! You must have gained another ten pounds!"

Pride craned his neck around as if in self-inspection and snorted his agreement. They all laughed. Then he thrust his head forward again and politely sniffed at Ashleigh and Samantha's pockets. "You're even looking for treats!" Ashleigh said with delight. "You know, I just might have something in here." She dug in her pocket and produced some broken pieces of carrot, which Pride gratefully accepted.

"Ashleigh," Mr. Townsend said, "I received some other very good news today." He pulled a folded piece of paper from his pocket. "A telegram to both of us from the Eclipse Award Committee. Pride has been named Horse of the Year."

Samantha thrust her fist in the air and let out a shout of joy. "All right, Pride!"

"Congratulations!" Tor said. "What great news!"

Ashleigh was reading the official telegram and looked up with a huge smile when she had finished. "To tell you the truth, Mr. Townsend," she said, "I would have been pretty upset if he hadn't gotten it— especially after all he's been through. No other horse deserves this honor as much as Pride."

Mr. Townsend laughed. "I agree, Ashleigh. There have been years where it's been a real toss-up over which horse to choose, but this wasn't one of them." He looked over at Pride. "I've been doing some thinking," he added. "I don't think there's any question now that he can't race another year."

"No," Ashleigh agreed, "I don't think so either. After what he's been through, it wouldn't be fair to him. And it will still be a while before he's totally back on his feet."

Mr. Townsend nodded. "If we're agreed on that, then I've also been thinking that it wouldn't be right to move him to Townsend Acres when he's ready to leave the clinic."

Ashleigh, Samantha, and Tor all turned to him.

Mr. Townsend continued. "I honestly don't think he could have pulled through if it hadn't been for the love, care, and encouragement he got from you and Sammy. In fact, I'm convinced of that. I saw how sick he was, and in all my years in the business, I've never seen a horse make a recovery when it was already so weak. I sincerely believe that I have you two to thank that he's still alive."

"We did what we did because we love him," Samantha said.

"Yes, I know," Mr. Townsend agreed. "And because of that I want him to stay at Whitebrook, where he can be near you both. It would be a huge draw for Townsend Acres to have a stallion of Pride's caliber actually standing at the farm, but I've seen for myself that the breeding facilities at Whitebrook are excellent. There is absolutely no reason why he can't stand as a stallion there, and Townsend Acres will still benefit and can take pride in the fact that he was bred at the farm." Mr. Townsend smiled. "Do you agree?"

"Agree?" Ashleigh said with a gasp. "Of course! It's what I've always wanted. Sammy too!"

"Then it's a deal," Mr. Townsend said. "When he's well enough, Pride goes *home* to Whitebrook."

Samantha felt such a wave of joy, her knees nearly buckled. "Thank you, Mr. Townsend! We'll take good care of him!"

"I haven't a doubt about that."

Samantha looked at Tor and saw the happy sparkle in his blue eyes. "A happy ending after all," he whispered.

She turned to Pride, who'd seemed to be listening alertly to their whole conversation. "Did you hear that, boy?" she asked, taking his head in her hands. "You're coming home to Whitebrook!"

Pride gently bobbed his head, then pressed his muzzle to Samantha's chest and whuffed contentedly.

Tor came up beside Samantha and said softly, "Maybe tonight's the night to finally celebrate your birthday. We have reason to now."

Samantha looked at him with a happy glow in her eyes. "You can say that again. What an unbelievable year!"